TWELVE DAYS DOWN

Alexander Crane

PROLOGUE

As I gripped the folder close to my chest I thought those scraps of paper inside were the only thing that would talk for me again. In the light and in the dark, I held that folder, sat on the sofa, eyes wide open, bubbles of moisture forming on my forehead. Waiting. Waiting for them to come. Not knowing who they were.

Then came the thud. The cracking splinter of wood. Determined footsteps in the hall. A figure striding to the curtains and tearing them open.

The winter day spread across the room. An image in the window came to me in pieces. It was you.

You stalked over and shook me and shouted at me. You shouted about a lot of things. I told you the answers were inside the folder that I clasped. That's when you snatched it from me.

You opened the folder and took out the pages that I'd written and read them sat on the windowsill; a grey silhouette in the pale light.

During those silent hours, I tried to ignore your

seething presence and face the end but all I could see was the start. Then the other moments of my life came back to me and at last I joined them together and could finally see that everything that had happened had led me to this point: rotting away in a single bedroom flat in London that I'd barely been able to leave for three months.

When I thought back to the beginning I saw black hair and tanned faces. The yellow circle in the spotless sky. The blue of the Black Sea. Running away from the tide; my mum lifting me into the air.

I was four years old when that summer ended. Nothing in my memory exists before. It was the first time I remember the sun hiding from my sight. It became dark in the afternoon and big blobs of rain would fall from the sky. At night I would lie in my mother's bed listening to the rain drumming off the shutters. Then the shouting would start downstairs and I'd feel scared all over again.

On Sundays, we'd go to a white building with a cross on the roof. I wore black trousers and polished shoes; a shirt and tie squeezed my neck. I sat alone with my mum on a wooden bench. My granddad and grandma and uncle and aunt and the rest of my family would sit far away. I didn't know why we didn't sit together.

When the rain stopped and it was warm again, all my family would pick grapes – all except my granddad. Instead he would sit on the porch, his face red and stomach fat. He didn't speak to me. He wouldn't look at me either.

When I asked my mum why he was always angry, she said, 'Because he drinks too many grapes.'

'Is that why he shouts at you, mummy?'

'No, he shouts at mummy because mummy did a bad thing.'

I didn't know that the bad thing that mummy had done was to have me.

Life continued in that way until I was seven. Then one night the shouting didn't stop. The next day my mum put our clothes into two suitcases. As she struggled down the dusty road, I followed, jumping between the cracks in the street and chasing the leaves that fluttered in the sea breeze. When we reached a bus stop, my mum sat on the bench and covered her face. An old man sitting next to her looked at her with sad eyes. He helped with the cases when the bus arrived, his aged arms barely able to place them on the luggage rack.

On the bus we passed fields of sunflowers, wound through small villages and towns, up towards the big green hills that seemed to touch the sky. Behind us the town of Ureki drifted silently into the past.

'Mummy, where are we going?'

'To live with your daddy in his country.'

'Is it far?'

'Yes, very far.'

The planes that I'd seen zooming over the Black Sea were a lot smaller than the ones at the airport. I didn't like the bigger planes - they were loud and made me feel sick.

Hours later the plane hit the ground with a bang. We collected our bags and put them in a black car. A man drove us through a strange place with no sea or grapes or sand. Just cars and red buses and tall buildings. My mum called the new place London. I wondered if all the big planes came here.

We slept in a small room in the same bed that night. When it was light my mum said she was leaving to visit my daddy. I was to stay in the room and not touch anything and not to answer the door.

After what seemed hours my mum returned. I ran to her crying. She picked me up.

Don't leave again.

I won't.

She was crying too. She cried all night.

The next day we got into another black car and went to a large building. Inside the large building were many small houses, one of which was owned by a woman called Aunt Tiesa. She was like my granddad and shouted at my mum all of the time.

'Mummy, when can I meet daddy?'

'You won't. It will just be us.'

'Why?'

'Because it will. Now listen, we shall never talk of him again. Promise?'

My mum kept that promise. So did I. And my dad, whoever he was and may be, wasn't mentioned again.

After that, we moved to a house in a place called Leeds. The house was made of red bricks and had a slated roof that was always wet. I didn't play outside anymore because my mum said there were too many cars. We painted things and cut paper to make dinosaurs instead. On Sundays we went to the park.

'Mummy, why on Sundays don't we go to the church anymore?'

'Because God is angry with us.'

'Why is God angry with us?'

'Because we are angry with him.'

I went to a special school for foreign people trying to

become English: my mum cleaned houses in a place called Harrogate. When I was eight I became so good at pretending to be English that I was allowed to go to a proper school. On my first day, I was made to stand up and tell them my name.

'My name is Zezva Chichinadze.'

'That's a nice name. Tell the class where you come from Zezva?' the teacher said.

'England.'

'No, before England.'

'My mummy says I am from England now.'

The teacher looked at me in the same way that the old man had looked at my mum at the bus stop. Her name was Miss Jenkins. She didn't ask me any more questions like that. I liked Miss Jenkins but soon had to leave her class and go to a new school. We left a lot in those days. We went to Doncaster, Sheffield and Nottingham. Sometimes we would live alone. Sometimes we lived with men called David, Kevin and Michael.

And on it went. My mum moved in with new boyfriends, falling into love and out of jobs, sleeping and cleaning her way through my childhood. Hard work and no luck, no man good enough for her little boy, the next place always the best. She could move house, areas and jobs. She could avoid boyfriends, colleagues, debts and friends. She could escape everything by running away. Everything except herself.

I was always the new boy with the strange name: fun to laugh at, too irrelevant to bully, not there long enough to like. But I was clever and rarely drew attention to myself by doing anything rash - such as talking or trying to make friends.

5

When I was ten I started to play football for the school team. The other boys had new shoes made from black leather. I wore my white gym shoes. But the boy with no boots was the best player so the other kids stopped laughing at him.

'Mum, why am I the only boy who doesn't have boots?'

'You do not need football boots Zezva. You need food and a house.'

And so it continued. At every school I joined the football team. Then the other kids liked me more and sometimes forgot my name and my shoes and all my other clothes.

'Mum, why am I the only boy still wearing shorts to school?'

'There is nothing wrong with being different.'

'Yes there is. Being different is embarrassing.'

When I was twelve I got a job on my mum's boyfriend's brother's farm: picking rocks out of fields, cleaning up animal shit, setting traps for the rats, etc. It allowed me to save up and buy the best boots I could. I became even better. It was at that time I decided it was safe to speak around the football team. When that went well I started to talk in class. I was surprised to discover I was one of those pupils who annoyed the teachers. I didn't punch or kick or spit like the other kids the teachers disliked. I did something far worse: I asked questions that they didn't know the answer to. The last thing they needed was a kid with a strange name ruining their lessons by asking about things that were not on the curriculum. I began to spend a lot of time on my own in the corridor.

Sometimes if I'd been in a place for a while I'd get

really confident and try an accent or some slang to fit in. I'd soon stop though when my mum scolded me in her perfect broken English, 'Zezva, a nice doctor or solicitor does not talk like this. Please talk correct.'

Never anywhere long enough to sign for a team, I gave up on being a footballer. If I couldn't make lots of money playing football I decided I'd do it another way. I was old enough to know that I didn't want to live the way we did anymore. Instead I started to study - and study harder than anyone else.

When my grades became really good I received an opportunity to go to New College, Oxford for an interview. I liked the sandstone turrets and the historical spires but wasn't too sure about the people that filled them. Although most appeared immune to my existence, one girl from Preston really took to me. She even asked for my email address. When I told her I didn't have one, she muttered something, excused herself and didn't speak to me again. I didn't know what her problem was; I didn't have an email address; no one had wanted it before. I couldn't understand why everyone was so concerned about things I didn't have. When they found out at school my house didn't have a TV the other kids seemed very concerned to point that out to me as well.

Whilst at Oxford I also met a gentle boy called Jeremy. He was baby-faced, had fluffy curls and dressed like an old man. Despite this he was very popular with the female interviewees. I didn't think the girls at my school would have liked Jeremy. Neither group of girls seemed to like me.

'I saw you talking to those girls last night. Did you get lucky?' I said to Jeremy the next morning in the food hall.

Questions like this had made me popular in the football team.

'Please,' Jeremy said with an exaggerated sniff. 'Not at breakfast.'

I didn't understand why it mattered it was breakfast but changed the subject all the same.

My final interview was with a white-bearded professor who had a deep voice. He asked me to reflect on the philosophy of conscious thought. I didn't have any reflections on it or any of the other questions he asked me.

When I returned to my school in the centre of Birmingham (miraculously we'd been there for over a year – a combination of my mum having secured herself a good job as a doctor's receptionist and not having secured herself a man), I was summoned to the headmaster's office.

'Zezva, you've not received a place at Oxford,' the headmaster said, unable to hide his glee. 'You'll naturally be disappointed. The reason given was that it was felt you were not rounded enough yet, especially in answering the questions about conscious thought.'

'I think you're a more rounded person if you don't know about conscious thought.'

The headmaster sighed. 'How on earth can that be the case?'

'If you know about stuff like that doesn't it mean that you spend too much time reading for someone your age? Shouldn't you be chasing girls or speeding in your new car or something?'

'This is exactly why you didn't get into Oxford. And exactly why you get in so much trouble in class. Your biggest problem, boy, is you don't accept what you are told. This is probably another reason why you'll not be going to Oxford.' He lowered his glasses and read the notes on his desks. 'One further criticism was that you appeared to be unused to intellectual discussion.'

'I tried to have one in class the other day and got sent here, remember?'

'Can you explain how criticising the geography teacher is an intellectual discussion?'

'We were talking about global warming and she had every light and radiator on in the classroom. When she asked for solutions it seemed obvious.'

'You didn't suggest that. You switched off the lights without permission. Then you turned the radiators off.'

'It was so naturally bright in there it took her five minutes to realise the lights were off.'

'The room was so dark no one could see a thing.'

'How did she see me turn the radiators off then?'

'Enough,' he shouted. 'Professor Ryman of New College has suggested that to overcome your many inadequacies you go on a gap year and re-apply next year.'

'What's a gap year?'

'It's when people suspend going to university and go travelling for a year.'

'None of my friends are doing that.'

'The people you associate yourself with Zezva are not the type that go on gap years. The people that go to Oxford are.' He tapped his pencil off the desk and pointed it at me. 'Take note.'

'How can they afford to go on holiday for a full year?'

'They get part-time jobs and save up.'

'What type of jobs?'

'Jobs like... working in cafés,' he floundered.

'There is no way you can afford to go on holiday for a full year working in a café. My mum worked in a café for two years and we didn't even go to Blackpool.'

'You're doing it again, Zezva. You'll get nowhere making all these problems with everything everyone says. That's probably another reason why you didn't get into Oxford.'

'I don't think anyone who works in a café goes on holiday for a year, that's all.'

'Well OK. Their parents give them money as well.'

'My mum won't give me money to travel for a year. She doesn't even like giving me the bus fare to come here. Wouldn't it just be better to work in a café and study the subject?'

'Of course not. Even if you do win a place next year you'll have nothing to talk about during freshers' week.'

'When do they talk about conscious thought?'

'In the weeks afterwards. They like to row too,' the headmaster said, pushing his glasses back up his nose, seemingly impressed by his own insightfulness.

My mum cried when I told her the news. I think she'd long given up on her own happiness so had decided to make me happy enough for both of us. Although she didn't know where to find contentment, she knew a number of places where she'd never discover it: the nine houses we'd lived in since moving to England for a start.

I tried to console her. 'Apparently if I go on holiday for a year and apply again, I might get in next year.'

'They did not say this, cruel boy,' she sobbed.

'They said if I go on holiday for a year I'll be a more rounded person.'

'And these teachers say they are intelligent. That's the worst advice I hear. You need to read more books not go on holiday.'

'I suggested that. But the headmaster said it would look bad on my CV if I read for a year and don't go on holiday for at least six months. I also wouldn't have anything to talk about in something called freshers' week.'

'Zezva, I will not forgive you for these unfunny jokes.'

She did, of course. And I didn't give in and worked even harder. When the A-level results came out I got grade As and went to York University to study Law. I found life very different. I discovered that many of the things that made you a loser at school like using big words, wearing different clothes and reading books made you popular at university. Students also did different things for attention. They rode small bikes and skateboarded rather than punching people who rode small bikes and skateboarded.

Most of my flat mates had brand new cars, stereos and game consoles. Despite this they were always competing over who had the least money or 'spends' as they called it. Whenever the contest started, I would lie because I'd been victorious in that game my whole life. The winner would usually declare their student loan spent within two weeks. They'd then do exactly the same things they'd been doing when they did have *spends*. I found the whole thing peculiar: I'd always presumed life was a competition to see who had the most money.

'Mum, please can I get a loan? Everyone else has one.'

'A loan from who?'

'The government.'

'They are the last person you will be wanting to have a loan from. These governments are worse than banks.'

'That's not true - it's not Georgia.'

'Yes I know. In Georgia the banks are worse.'

So I worked in a café instead. It didn't teach me anything about conscious thought. I couldn't afford a holiday either.

I played football for the university first team and won player of the year twice. I think I was popular with my teammates and even some of their female friends. But I seldom went out drinking with the team. I needed to work hard and take my chance. My flat mates used to laugh at me for my diligence but they didn't understand. If they were successful they'd go back to the lifestyle they'd always had. If they were failures they'd go back to the lifestyle they'd always had. My main motivation to succeed was my mother. If I got a job with a big law firm perhaps she'd be happy again.

I achieved a first class degree, completed the Legal Practice Course with distinction and finished my training contract with a regional firm in Manchester. Once I was a qualified solicitor, at the age of twenty-four, I accepted a role with a large London firm in the corporate department.

Two weeks after moving to London I met my girlfriend Shell. She didn't really speak about her past but seemed quite angry about it. She directed all her anger towards the wider injustices of life; she found plenty of things to be annoyed about. She became a protester, activist and all-round humanist. I think the only thing she wanted more than to save the world was to make people notice she was saving the world.

When I first met her I was infatuated. She was argumentative and had a mean streak - which I was surprised to find attractive. She also had a pretty face, big breasts and a strong, in your face, sexuality - which I was less surprised to find attractive. The only thing that annoyed me was that she tried to change me all the time.

The main change Shell pursued was for me to quit the corporate lifestyle and become an activist like her. She told me I'd help more people that way. I guessed I agreed but not strongly enough that I wanted to become poor again. I didn't really care about politics back then; I wanted to do the best I could with my own life without bothering others. In any case I didn't know if I could make anything better. I had enough problems making my mum happy, let alone the whole world.

When my mum heard about Shell she asked me four hundred questions. Is she good to her mum? What does her father do? Has she any brothers or sisters? Are they in jail? And so on...

With all the right answers, she decided that she loved Shell before she'd met her. When she did, she loved her even more.

Just when we were all easing into our new life, something happened. I can't... even now. My mum. A car. A crash. She died that night.

After the funeral I decided it was best to pretend the whole thing hadn't happened. I wasn't very good at it and felt sad and missed her every day. I still do. I always will.

I think that Shell felt duty bound to stay with me. A couple of months after it happened she started to avoid me. But the more she distanced herself, the more I clung on.

It wasn't until the following summer at the age of twenty six that everything fell apart. Three months later I started to see Dr O'Brien. The esteemed therapist found me a difficult patient. It used to particularly wind him up when I answered his questions with questions. He'd made a living out of doing that - the last thing he needed was some patient stealing his best trick.

Predictably he was very interested in my childhood and family. It didn't take him long to decide what the sources of my problems were.

'It's all down to your upbringing.'

'In what way?'

'You don't know where you come from.'

'I do,' I assured him. 'I come from Georgia.'

'You had a disappointing childhood. You didn't settle.'

'Maybe I'd have been more disappointed if I had settled.'

'You won't forgive your mum for the way things were.'

'You're right. There is nothing to forgive.'

'OK, Mr Chichinadze.' O'Brien lifted up my notes and straightened them on his desk. 'We seem to be getting nowhere. Why don't you tell me why you think that you are here?'

I couldn't avoid it any longer so told him it was all down to a series of events that happened three months before. I said at that time my girlfriend Shell didn't seem to like me anymore. I'd also decided I didn't like my job. I had only done it to make my mum happy and she was dead now. But despite it all I was still coping until a period at the end of the summer. Even then I handled everything that was thrown at me. I was fine until I made the stupidest mistake of my life: I started to hope.

O'Brien reluctantly gave up the childhood angle and, perhaps eager to get rid of me, he concluded that all my problems had come together in a short space of time and had caused me to suffer from, 'an acute, time-limited psychotic episode followed by a major depressive episode.'

I said that all this talk of episodes made it sound like the whole thing was available in box set. Why didn't he stop hiding behind the technical language and just say he thought that I was bonkers?

O'Brien looked stern and said that he didn't approve of the word bonkers. He then tried to get us back on track by asking me, in the calmest voice he could manage, to recount the events of that late summer. At last, I said, once you hear about this you'll know I'm not crazy and if I am, it's not my or my mother's fault.

O'Brien told me he didn't like the word crazy either. He also said to stop shouting and waving my arms around. I told him I wasn't and kept on talking. He looked scared and asked me to calm down. He said that a lot - unnecessarily in my opinion. He advised I go away for a month and write down everything that had happened to me. I'm sure the main reason he suggested this was because he didn't want to see me for a month.

To his relief (and ultimate disappointment) I returned a month later with a folder of typed pages. I told him I'd narrowed down my problems to twelve specific days that all took place in about a three week period, three months before.

He said he'd read it and asked me to come back in a week.

When I returned he gazed at me with a strange look in his eye; a look I hadn't seen for a long time: I hoped it was understanding; perhaps it was despair.

I left his surgery and didn't see him again. Instead I drew the curtains and barricaded myself in the house. Days passed. Perhaps weeks. I sat in the same place, on the sofa, clinging onto those pages that I typed for Dr O'Brien.

That was the folder I was clutching when you kicked down the door and burst into the house. That was the folder that you ripped from my grasp. You were the first person I'd seen since O'Brien. You seemed so angry. I daren't speak: I didn't know what to say.

When you finished reading its contents, you exhaled deeply and looked at me. 'Is it all true?'

'I don't know,' I said, 'but it is my truth.'

Here is what you read.

DAY 1

It all started in a bar called Ricky's: the self-proclaimed centre of radical thought in London. Inside, fine artists mixed with graffiti artists; ballet dancers with moshers; vampires with Goths. Different people that all believed the same: that things needed to change and soon. My girlfriend, Shell, agreed and also agreed that Ricky's was her favourite place in the world.

Beyond the hype, Ricky's was a small dimly lit bar. I've spent many unhappy times in that place but that night pierces my conscience to this day. Perhaps it was the final moment of delusion; a negative epiphany of what my life had become and was going to be. Or maybe it was just the starting point of those twelve days that changed everything.

*

I took one step inside. Zoom. The joint impact of eyes and temperature scorched me with their disapproval. Slam. The door swung shut behind me. The last swish of the night air. My shirt and tie noosed my neck; physical and social strangulation. Casting glances in every direction, I tried to find the people that I wish I'd never found in the first place. There they were. Recognition sunk to my feet. My suit clung to my body as I made my way between the tables towards them. Trip, stumble, whack, pardon, sorry to be a bother.

Reaching the table, not even the coldness of the reception could chill my burning discomfort. I dragged a seat next to Shell and sat down. There was no greeting, just a spark of disapproval in the depths of those dark eyes. She looked away to the candle in the centre of the table, her lip ring glistening in the amber glow.

Before I could ask her what was wrong, a man nicknamed Sparky caught my attention with a wave. It was more mocking than welcoming. With his mop of auburn curls, peach-fuzz beard and green eyes he thought he was really suave.

'Hello Zezva.' He reclined in his chair and rested his hands behind his head. 'How was another day being… that guy?'

'What guy?'

He looked me up and down and smirked. 'You know, a *you* type of guy.'

I was unsure what he was talking about but was certain of one thing: as usual I was under attack. I turned to Shell, 'Is this his way of starting a conversation?'

She rolled her eyes, 'He's taking the piss.'

'Why?'

'Your suit. You know people in here don't like them.'

'They don't like a piece of cloth?'

'Exactly,' Shell said.

When Shell said, "exactly" the argument was over with her declared the winner. I didn't say that it was a bit unreasonable for her friends to dislike a type of cloth. I didn't say a lot of things back then.

I inadvertently locked eyes with a scowling woman sitting opposite.

'That thing you have on,' she said, gesturing at her chin. 'Are you made to wear that at work, like a uniform?'

'I suppose.'

'Like...why?'

'I work as a lawyer. I have to dress smartly.'

'What like a human rights lawyer or something?'

'No, as a corporate lawyer,' Sparky said, somehow reclining even further in his seat.

Again I said nothing. What could I say? It was true. I didn't know if it was something to be ashamed of or not.

When I first applied to law firms I learnt they were seeking a person who was motivated and flexible, with the correct personal attributes and academic qualifications. Luckily I was flawed enough to be perfect. In terms of flexibility I had attended about twenty different schools when I was younger so had no regional loyalty. I also had ideal results: I'd done well academically, but not well enough to lead to the suspicion I might try to think for myself. My motivation was also unquestionable: I had massive debts and the taste of childhood poverty bestowing me with the desperation that eighteen years of peasantry brings. They knew that once sucked in there wasn't much chance of someone like me leaving. With these skills, training and lifestyle all the big firms had fought over who would receive the privilege of wrecking my life. It was a contest I don't think anyone won.

'Sparks, when you on?' Shell said, not even trying to hide she was changing the subject from the inconvenience of her boyfriend's job title.

'Any second, I best go get ready.' Sparky got up and flounced off with his guitar.

Seeing my chance, I whispered in Shell's ear, 'Quick

let's go. He won't notice.'

'No way. Sparky is genius. We're staying.'

As my head dropped to the floor, I noticed Sparky's dog sat under his chair. His hair was coarse yet fluffy like the tangled fur of an old teddy bear. Breathing lethargically he looked like he wanted to die. He must have been in Ricky's bar for a while.

Possibly he sensed my pity, perhaps we caught eyes, maybe it was love at first sight. For whatever reason he shuffled over to me, sniffed my leg and rested next to my chair.

An hour went by and seeped into two. Just when the indie tributes, protest songs and attempted rock anthems had started to merge into one nasal whine, with a theatrical flourish Sparky flogged his guitar one last time before crashing it onto the ground and strutting off the stage.

*

Out the door, touched by a smile, I burst back into the world and hurried towards the car. I reached it and rested my arms on the roof, the cool air seeping through my shirt, fanning the uneasy remains of the night. I reached down to unlock the door but instead felt a wet sensation brushing my hand. It was the dog's black button nose.

'Look,' I said. 'It snuck out of the door and followed me all the way down the street. He loves me.'

'No, he doesn't.' Shell said. 'I brought him out.'

'Oh,' I said, glancing down at the mongrel. 'Why?'

'We're going to look after him for Sparky for a few weeks as a favour.'

'A few weeks?! What does he think we are? A kennel?'

'You were in love with that thing when you thought it was following you. Now it's Sparky's decision and you hate it,' she said, her words annoying me because they were true. 'Anyway, don't be so inconsiderate. The poor guy has moved into a very expensive house with really pricey furniture. This dog isn't house trained. You can't expect Sparky to look after it with the cost of all his things.'

'What about my things?!'

'Oh that's just family stuff, passed down for generations that your aunt gave to you. It doesn't matter if he damages them. Anyway, you're terrible not liking dogs.'

'I do like dogs. I just don't like his dog,' I said. I tried to sound angry but was distracted by the adorable creature pawing at my leg. 'What's his name?'

'I don't know,' said Shell. 'What shall we call him? We should think of something really unique.'

'Let's just call him the Dog.'

'We can't call him that. It's cruel.'

'I can't think of anything nicer to call him,' I said. 'That's what he is, plus it is unique. How many dogs do you know called The Dog?'

That puzzled her. 'If we call him The Dog can he come with us?'

'OK, fine,' I said, picking him up and opening the car door. I felt a lot better as I placed him in the back seat; not only was I getting to keep him but I could also pretend to Shell that I didn't want to in the process.

I opened the door and settled into the driver's seat. The night already seemed a distant memory as I started the engine. Control and command replaced the imbalance that overcame me every time I entered that bar. I pulled away and Ricky's began to fade away in my rear view mirror.

I drove and listened to Shell going on about how Sparky's genius lay in his contradictions. Apparently he was strong yet vulnerable; off-hand yet intimate; intense but fun.

After ten minutes of listening to this nonsense, I pulled up outside a row of townhouses masquerading as apartment blocks. I glanced up to the top floor flat that we loosely called home. When I looked around it the estate agent had described it as Victorian; I thought he meant in terms of architectural prowess rather than degenerative quality.

I killed the engine and turned to look at Shell. It was dark now, only the street lights illuminating the street. But as I sat there I felt that somewhere above the topmost branches, over the highest buildings, through the clouds, up into the stratosphere, space and beyond, that the moon was shining on us. And with that feeling I viewed her with affection. OK, she'd been pretty horrible to me lately. Yes, she could be cantankerous and selfish and temperamental. True, she also seemed to be avoiding me. But I still found her so challenging, so radiant, so alive.

'Right, do you want to stay over?'

'Very funny,' she said but there was laughter in her voice. 'I live here remember.'

'I keep forgetting... despite all that rent money you keep pumping into my account.'

She slapped my bicep with the back of her hand. 'You said that you didn't want any money.'

'I don't.' I leant across and kissed her on the cheek. 'I'm just messing with you.'

We got out of the car and moved towards the house. Entering the porch we did that thing that couples do as we laughed at our run-of-the-mill banter. The joke that only we understood symbolised a togetherness that only we could comprehend; the laughter an expression of the bliss that such glorious isolation brings. Linking her arm and strolling into the hallway, a feeling of contentment washed over me and manifested itself in the type of smile that is often seen on poor bastards who mistakenly believe they are in love.

DAY 2

I walked into the living room across the frayed carpet and slumped onto our couch. It was designed with the faded patterns of flowers - what it lacked in style it didn't make up for in comfort. I manoeuvred between the lumps and started to do up my tie.

Attiisshhu.

I glared at the curtains that seemed to inhale, swallow and store every particle of dust.

They weren't even the room's worst feature. If our furniture impressed anything it was that all ancient belongings can't be classed as antiques. In fact the entire house looked like one of those exhibits entitled, 'How the Edwardians Used to Live.' It was my Aunt Tiesa's fault. In her later years she combined her two favourite interests: hypochondria and clairvoyance. Foretelling the imminence of her own death, she changed her will to bequeath to me all her unassigned chattels - technically known as the dregs. When a moustached doctor accused her of contriving her latest ailment, she died to prove him wrong, like any proud old woman would, wearing a knowing smile across her wrinkled face.

All this coincided with moving into my own flat. My mum said how lucky I was whilst warning me it would be disrespectful to the dead if I didn't let all of Tiesa's things ruin my new house. So here they were, doing exactly that.

The empty birdcage with its rusted prongs was probably the most archaic of all the discards. Or maybe it was the gold-plated clock with its timeless chiming.

Not to be outdone my mum also gifted us a white woollen rug she'd picked up from a flea market in Croydon. It didn't match anything either, so in a way suited the look of the room. The house had also come with some complimentary qualities such as damp ceilings, crumbling plaster and a defective boiler. These gifts were either the fault of the landlord or the builders depending on who you spoke to last - it was nice of them to share the credit.

This combination of death, misplaced generosity and erosion had somehow managed to endow the house with the ambience of intellect. It smelt like it was inhabited by two aged teachers. In truth, the apartment was enveloped by a good, old-fashioned ignorance; an intellectual vacuum that sucked in all four of its bookless rooms.

Looking around at Tiesa's bequests, I wished I wasn't so sentimental or had a girlfriend materialistic enough to force me not to be. I could then throw it all out, filling the space with plastic pine tables and faux leather sofas; at least then we would be fashionable in our tastelessness.

I finished tying my tie and followed the sound of slurping to see the Dog underneath the bridge table. He was devouring what seemed to be a bowl of cornflakes and milk.

I got up and went into the kitchen to find Shell. She was lounging at the table, an open tub of butter strewn to her left, knife cast to her right, breadcrumbs scattered across the work top. She wasn't exactly the home-maker; you could trace her every move by following her trail of inconsideration. Ignoring me, she flicked through a magazine, a cigarette loosely held in her left hand.

She hadn't made me anything: breakfast for one was her specialty. I decided to have a bowl of cereal and opened the fridge, only to be faced by an empty milk bottle.

'Have you used the last of the milk?'

'No, it was the Dog.'

'The Dog? Let itself in and poured some itself did it?'

'I can't believe you are begrudging the poor thing a simple breakfast when he's so depressed.'

'Shell, dogs can't be depressed.'

'Don't be stupid. Of course they can.'

I slammed the fridge door shut. 'Tell you what I'll book him in for a therapy session. Shall I take him there or leave the car keys and let him drive himself?'

'You're very strange sometimes.' Her eyebrows rippled a frown across her whole forehead. 'What are you on about?'

'Nothing,' I said, deciding to leave our daily argument until later.

I went back into the living room and picked up my house keys. As I walked out I looked at the Dog. He actually did look sad. Really sad.

*

I trudged down the steps to meet a silent platform. Billboards tarred the walls with corporate graffiti, boasting of the latest must see, must read, must listen to piece of art. The workforce glared anonymously ahead, cocooning themselves from the rest of humanity with their headphones and icy expressions.

A distant trundle. A warm draft of dormant air. The

train stopped. People seeped out. Others weeped in. The doors clamped shut. A moment of intimacy with all those strangers. The telephonist reading a self-help book flanked the smiling banker, talking to the hapless merchant, next to the over-competent junior. The genius who threw it all away trapped the arm of the salesman who couldn't sell anything. Millionaires pressed against failures, ageless people with seven, six, five, ten years' experience, investing in everything but themselves.

The train slowed. Hiss, whispered the hydraulics. Click, slid the doors. Out we pushed. Stomp, we marched, a million cream tiles concaved overhead, one for every polished footstep. People barged out, desperate to get their spreadsheet fix. Quick, shouted their feet, not a millisecond to spare. The escalators chugged, the barriers ticked. Out we burst. A man swung his pink FT. A woman with wet hair bustled past. Two magpies scavenged for morsels. Flap, they panicked, as a man barked into his mobile phone. A renegade broke file crouching to rearrange his briefcase; tutting side steps, shaking heads, a millisecond lost, never to return. Their pace quickened, not a flicker of expression touching their faces, as they passed below the grey oblongs of enterprise; that silhouetted block chart eating into the heavens above.

*

I reached my destination. The last glance up. The sky was like nothing that day, just a blank sheet of paper crumpled over the city. The revolving door swung round and round. The squeaky foyer floor. A regimented nod to the security guards. I dashed for the packed elevator. Why didn't I wait? Insufferably busy; the underground in a microcosm. As the doors were shutting, Mandy from

Human Resources jammed her way in. 'Room for a small one?' she bawled. Swaying like a prize fighter, I tried to avoid her line of vision but achieved the opposite effect: my movement only seemed to draw her attention.

'Alright Zezva, how are you?'

'Fine, thank you,' I mumbled.

'Nice tie. I love a spot of pink.' She cackled at her own joke. 'Do anything at the weekend?'

'No, not much.'

'Not what I heard. My brother saw you. Said that you were hammered, mate. Said that you were being sick all over the club.'

I didn't go to clubs. I barely drank. I suppose that was the joke. But those people in the lift didn't know that. The glower of all those eyes; sweat forming; pins prickling my skin. I embarrass easily. I guess, that was the joke also.

Bing. The first stop. To my relief, out stepped Mandy. She couldn't resist saying over her shoulder, 'See you later boozy.'

The lift continued upwards, stopping at each floor allowing people to shuffle out muttering 'sorry' and 'excuse me' on their way. The last people left were me and Howard. There was not much to say about Howard. Married to his wife and his job, Howard had cultivated an impassive personality that gave the impression of clinical professionalism.

'Did you hear that Mandy?' I said to him. 'Why do people talk in lifts?'

'You're doing it now,' he said, staring forward.

It was true, I was. But did he need to point it out?

Howard was generally considered to be unusual and hard to fathom, but I saw him as an open book;

unfortunately the pages were blank.

We exited the lift and walked towards our desks. The banter lulled and silence crept across the floor. Some people can enter a room and make everyone feel uncomfortable. Howard managed to have that effect on an entire office.

That's what I thought. When I think about it now, it was probably me that had that effect on the entire office.

I didn't have time to think about that because I had an urgent job. I logged on my computer, opened the internet and searched for, 'dogs and depression.' And there they were: hundreds of articles on the depressed dogs of the world. Shell was right! And The Dog was back in the house by itself suffering from this affliction. Maybe I should go home and –

'What are you doing Zezva?'

I minimised the webpage and turned in my seat to face the head of my department. 'Hi, Hugh.'

Hugh was fifty years old, thin, bald, bespectacled and belligerent. His child-like physique complemented his adult-sized ego. When you talked to him at his desk he would recline back, mixing deep exhalations with thunderous yawns, letting you know a man of his position couldn't be more relaxed about speaking to someone in yours. 'Were you reading an article about dogs and suicide?' he said.

'Me?' I said, pointing into the centre of my chest.

He looked at me like who else do you think I'm talking to.

'Yes, the Suicidal Dogs,' I said. 'They're a band. I'm thinking of seeing them.'

'The Suicidal Dogs? Yes, I know them. I think I saw

29

them at Glasto last year.'

'Glasto?'

'Glastonbury, Zezva. The Festival.' He raised an eyebrow and opened his body to draw Howard into the conversation. 'And this guy is meant to be young!'

How Howard laughed. How he had no choice.

The now friendly Howard was bombarding Hugh with various questions about, 'The Festival.' I phased out and it all blended into a loop of fake laughter and words like 'splendid', 'jolly', 'magnificent.' I gradually turned my chair back towards my screen. Just when I thought I'd removed myself from *convo* about *Glasto*, I realised Hugh was saying my name.

I turned back to face him. 'Sorry what did you say?'

'That there are department drinks tonight,' Hugh said. 'Three line whip. My treat.'

He was so desperate to show off, he'd even invited me.

*

The hosting bar was well-lit and spacious. Modern art was placed throughout the stylish interior. A pianist played soothing tunes that seemed to explore the tenderness of new love. The notes melodically caressed the fragranced air. It was the antidote to the drab of Ricky's. I couldn't decide which was worse.

The area the firm had booked was cordoned off with yellow and black ticker tape. It resembled a crime scene. It appeared to be a cynical attempt to promote 'networking.'

Approaching two leather sofas I could hear my colleagues were already playing their favourite game: *Who Can Be the Most Dull*. The competition was fierce. I placed the tray of drinks on the table and sat down.

'Alright Zezva. Bet that's the first round you've ever got in.....at the free drinks event....,' a colleague called Blackie said. His slicked-back hair exposed his face in all its sneering splendour. Sure, I went to a comprehensive school but it didn't hold me back, said his crocodile shoes. My dad was a self-made millionaire, replied his salmon coloured shirt. I'm a bit of a geezer, interrupted his red braces.

'Bang on time actually. I was just talking about a deal I did last week. £350million refinancing of a little soft drinks company,' he said, immune to my attempts to ignore him.

'Added bonus; it's a great story too,' I said.

'Oh sorry big shot, what's the biggest deal you've done?'

'You didn't do the deal. You wrote the deal down on a big piece of paper that the people actually doing the deal didn't see until they wrote their names on the back page.'

His face reddened. 'You know I'm about to get promoted, do you? Well, when I'm your boss I'll remember that's the value you think we add.'

The ring of my phone saved me. I walked away and answered without excusing myself.

'Hi, I have some bad news, I'm locked out,' Shell said. Her gleeful tone didn't match her words.

'How did that happen?'

'I left my keys in the house. Tell you what - I'll come to meet you.'

'Absolutely not. Where are you?

'Outside. I can see you,' she said, with a wicked laugh.

I looked out of the window. She was staring back at me through the glass with her phone pressed against her ear. She hadn't forgotten to wear her spiky bag covered with badges or her red and black striped tights. I thought she'd been asking a lot of questions when I told her about this drinks event.

I waved back to her and goodbye to my career.

*

Leaving the bar, I waited until we were out of earshot before I said, 'OK, right, let's start with the most obvious. What was the point in starting that argument?'

Shell's brow creased. 'That Blackie guy is going to waste his life thinking about money. I was pointing out that it won't fulfil him.'

'Of course it will fulfil him, that's all he cares about.'

'Well, you have to try.'

'You need to accept people don't change'

'Some do.'

'What does that mean?'

A moment's pause worth a hundred words. 'Nothing,' she mumbled. 'Anyway, he'll see the light after he meets all my friends.'

'When is that going to happen?'

'I've invited Blackie to Sparky's full moon party.'

'You did what? You know how much I'm dreading that party and now you've made it worse.'

'I thought it would give you someone to talk to...'

Her bottom lip was thrust out, the double studs of her piercing glinting in the street light. She looked genuinely upset with me. I nudged her and then threw my arm over her shoulder; you couldn't fault her spirit and she was certainly consistent in enforcing her views upon people. 'It's no big deal. I'm not bothered if he comes. Anyway, when we meet your parents tomorrow I can get my own back.'

'Please don't joke about it.' I felt her body tense. 'I'm only agreeing to meet them because you keep on going on about it. You know we don't get along.'

In truth, I didn't know whether they got on or otherwise. We hadn't met. Although she was the first girl I'd lived with, and we'd been together for nearly two years, I didn't really know Shell at all. I knew she was four years younger than me, twenty two; she'd not been to university, and that she came from London. And that was more or less it. Every piece of information about her past was treated like an earth-shattering revelation. Perhaps tomorrow more would be revealed about the disguised girl that I had my arm around.

And with that thought we arrived at the tube station I had left thirteen hours before. Another circle joined in the sphere of my life.

DAY 3

A haze of movement, dancing through the crowds, a stride becomes a jog; too late to walk: too many people watching to sprint. I'm late but I'm cool, says my motion; move faster or she'll kill you, yells my mind.

Into a building and under an archway that reads, 'Apple Market.' Not a core in sight. Instead a collection of stalls and shops selling everything you don't need and more; the larder of London, digested by the consumer revolution. Black lanterns hang from the rafters, shining over the popcorn stand, the smell of melted sugar sweetening the cosmetic staleness.

A corridor lined with red-brickwork, arched doors, designer clothes and beautiful girls to adore. Neck scarves, leather gloves, patterned suits, modernity born, bearing new fruit. Tented stalls, green striped awnings, nautical jewellery, salesgirls fawning. Outside now, not far to go, past the cafes and the slurps of latte.

Mirth belts from those drinking on the balcony above, a triangular roof behind them, Covent Garden engraved on the sandstone. Under the arch stands a woman, her red hair spiked, arms folded.

*

I wilted against a pillar, furiously panting, my head

resting against my arm.

'Don't think this little act is going to get you off, Zezva.' she said. 'Where have you been? You were meant to be here at 12:30.'

'Sorry I took a short cut through that market, there are more people in there than China,' I said, wiping imaginary sweat from my brow.

'Well, there is no point going anymore. Let's go home.'

'Relax we'll only be a few minutes late. It's your parents not a job interview.'

'It'll give them an excuse to have a go at me.'

'If they're looking for an excuse they will probably start with the way you are dressed,' I said, stepping back and studying her attire. 'Is black the new black or something? What's with all the jewellery? And when did your hair become red?'

'This morning.'

'Why?'

'They need to accept who I am.'

'Shell, you don't need to dress up to prove yourself to them.'

'OK, fine let's go,' she said, flattening her hair slightly with her hand.

We walked the short distance to the restaurant, went inside and waited to be seated. The room was softly lit with tangerine-coloured walls. Recognition struck. I'd been here with work. This place was mind-blowingly expensive.

'Will I have to pay for this?' I said.

'No, they'll pay.'

'Is it safe to offer out of politeness?'

'What do you mean?'

'If I offer to pay will there be no way that they'll take

me up on the offer?'

'No, they'll pay. They're loaded. You could offer to pay for the wine or something.'

'Do you know how much wine costs in these places? I may as well offer to take them on holiday.'

'It's not a big deal, Zezva. Just be tight as usual or whatever.'

Before I could respond we were interrupted by a beaming hostess. 'Good afternoon. Table for two?'

'No, we're meeting people,' I said. Her tanned skin, high cheek-bones and curled dark hair seemed unusual yet familiar.

'Of course, follow me. We find them together,' she said with a smile.

In the furthest corner sat Shell's parents. The mother was plump with a slightly stooped posture and greying hair. When she spotted Shell she got up, a magnificent smile adding a sparkle to her eyes.

Her father remained seated. His hair was neatly combed and he was clean shaven. He wore a shirt and tie combination even though it was the weekend. He looked like a father should: dependable, consistent and socially embarrassing.

'Hello darling, how are you?' the mother said, giving Shell a hug.

'Good to see you, Michelle,' her father said. 'And this must be Zuzermar?' he gambled.

I nodded - when everyone your entire life can't pronounce your name you learn to agree.

After the customary introductions, we sat down to spend what I suspected would be an hour of pleasant small talk. Soon we were on topic and I eased into the predictable conversation.

'Wasn't it busy out there Sesermar?' Joan said, her attempt to pronounce my name worse than John's. 'The city is really changing.'

'Yes it is,' I said. 'Sorry, that's why we're a bit late. I got caught in the market.'

'Not a wise short cut,' John said.

'Never mind you're here now,' Joan said. 'You'll get to know the city soon.'

Shell's face tensed. 'He's not fresh off the boat! He's lived in London for five years.'

It was two years actually. But Shell wasn't to know that – it would have involved listening to me.

'Also his name is Zezva. Zez-va.'

The waitress approached, expertly ignored the conversation and placed the scroll menus in front of us. I unravelled the scroll to reveal handwritten Italian, etched by the most precise of quills.

'Shall we start with wine? Is a nice white OK?' John said.

Fine, we agreed.

'Zezva said he would pay for the wine,' Shell said, concealing a smirk. I gave an admiring nod. The spiteful bitch had got me on this one.

'Don't be silly,' John said.

'He's a solicitor,' Shell said. 'He can afford it.'

Joan started to nudge John with her elbow. 'A solicitor? You didn't mention that Shell. What a good job.'

'Yes, well done,' John said. 'You must have done very well at school. Which one did you go to?'

'Quite a few actually. You won't have heard of any of them.'

'Oh not one of the big names then. Shell's brother Charlie - who is at Oxford - went to Westminster School.'

'Did you go to Oxford, Sesermar?' Joan said.

'No. York.'

'Well, it's still a good university,' John said. 'Michelle didn't go to university.'

Shell dropped her menu and glared at her dad. 'Why bring that up?'

'I was only saying, darling,' John said, fidgeting in his seat. 'Do you have a job yet?'

'I do workshops in the community and prison.'

'In prison?' Joan said, slapping her hand into the middle of her chest. 'Working with criminals?'

'I suppose it's good news that you're finally working,' John said. 'Does it pay well?'

'You would ask that wouldn't you, Dad. If you must know it's voluntary.'

'Oh Shell I can't finance you forever and I'm sure Zuzermar could do with some help with the mortgage.'

'I rent at the moment,' I corrected.

'Oh dear,' Joan said, her expression becoming more pained. All this talk of prisons and renting houses was really getting to her. 'You should really buy a house. It's a great investment for the future. We've already told Shell we'll help her with any deposit. Perhaps you two could buy together?'

'NO!' Shell bawled.

Her reply was so unexpected it took a second to sink in. Perhaps she didn't understand that her mother had offered to give her thousands of pounds.

'Come on Michelle, we're trying to help,' John said.

'It's Shell,' she retorted, ringing her napkin in her

hands, furious that her father had had the temerity to call her the name he'd given her. I could see the all too familiar kindling in her dark eyes.

'What do you both do for a living?' I said, attempting to move us away from the argument.

'I'm the Financial Director of an oil company and Michelle's, sorry, Shell's mother is an accountant,' John said, never taking his eyes from his daughter.

On cue, the friendly waitress returned and began pouring the bottle of wine, her thumb pressed against the punt, her fingers barely touching the walls of its body. In the history of crushed grapes never had wine been poured at a slower pace.

'It doesn't change, does it?' Shell said, deciding now was the perfect time to re-start the row. 'Going on about university and jobs and houses.'

'Wine?' the waitress asked me, doing a brilliant impression of impasse.

'No thank you,' I said. Although I desperately wanted a drink, I reasoned my refusal would make her leave quicker.

'Zuzermar, why aren't you drinking?' John said.

'Oh picking on my boyfriend now. Is he not good enough for you either?' Shell yelled. As her voice rang around the room I contemplated how much the wine refusal had backfired.

'Please give me a drink,' I pleaded with the waitress.

In response to my change of heart John did what all kindly fathers would do in such an awkward situation: he made it worse by trying to help. He picked up my glass and plunged it in the direction of the waitress who still had the wine bottle in the most delicate of grips. John's outstretched arm collided with the bottle. It slipped out of her hand, fell to the stone floor and smashed instantly. Wine and shards of glass covered Shell's leather boots.

Silence descended – the restaurant was too posh for the customary ironic cheer.

'Vakh. Rogor damivarda,' the waitress squealed.

'Araushavs, ar inerviulo,' I comforted. 'Sheni brali ar ikho.'

Meanwhile the chilled chardonnay had done little to douse the inevitable combustion from Shell. She got up and kicked her chair in anger. Thud, it hit the floor. She glared at her father, stormed away from the table, out of the restaurant and her parents' lives.

'Michelle, wait. It was an accident,' her dad called after her.

We sat motionless, each trying to comprehend what had happened. The waitress finished scraping the glass into a pan, curtseyed and scurried away.

'W-w-what language was that, Zuzermar?' John said, trying to regain his composure, his Adams apple gulping up and down his neck.

'It was Georgian. That's where I was born.'

'Oh I thought you looked...I mean, I thought your name was a bit... a bit,' he floundered before giving in, 'a bit foreign.'

'John, stop pretending that nothing has happened.' Tears formed in Joan's eyes. 'I told you not to bring up the job thing.'

His fist thudded off the table, sending high pitched vibrations through the cutlery. 'DON'T YOU BLAME ME I....' He glanced in my direction, coughed and then straightened his tie. 'I'm sorry Zuzermar. You must think we're a terrible family.'

'She did that last time too. Getting angrier and angrier and then finding an excuse to leave. I don't know why she can't stand us,' Joan said. 'She had everything growing up. And when she started dressing in that way we loved her as much as when we dressed her as a child.'

'I don't know what's happened to her or why she's so angry. She's been arrested before, you know. I never thought I'd see my daughter an anarchist.' John leant forward and touched my shoulder. White hairs sprouted from the back of his hand. 'Please look after her.'

'For us,' Joan added.

'I will... Listen, I'd better go after her.' I stood up and pushed my seat under the table. 'She cares you know. I'm sure she'll come back to you.'

Her father managed a sort of smile; more a grimace lightened by a glimmer of hope.

Outside on the street, I shielded my eyes from the spit of the darks clouds. A plague of tourists bustled past heading towards the indoor market and away from the imminent downpour. Further down the street they passed a figure sat on the kerb. She was slumped forward, her head in hands. I walked to her and she glanced up, her face softer than before, her dark eyes like two burned out coals.

I sat down next to her, just out of striking distance. 'How are you?'

'Fine.'

'Good. Let's go back inside.'

'I can't.'

'The wine thing was an accident.'

'You really think it was the wine, Zezva?'

'Your parents are still in the restaurant.'

'What did they say when I left? I bet they were slagging me off.'

'Of course they weren't.'

The rain grew heavier. The deluge filtered into a stream, flowing through the gap between us into the gutter and down the drain.

'Did you notice all they wanted to talk about was what school and university you went to and what job you have?'

'They were making small talk.'

'No, they were putting off asking me about my life because it upsets them so much.'

'Shell, some people don't have parents. And you hate yours, for what? Giving you the perfect start in life and wanting you to take advantage of it.'

'Do you know what it feels like for your parents to not accept you? To disapprove of everything you are?'

'Well they aren't going to stop being disappointed with you if you act like that, are they?'

'You really have no idea why I acted like that do you?' she said, searching in my eyes for an empathy that I didn't have. 'I knew I wouldn't be able to talk to you about this. You can't be objective after...'

'After what?'

'After,' she bit her lip. 'You know, your mum and everything.'

I could feel the sensation of each cold drop of rain; the water running down my face; the taste of hair product on my lips. 'That's exactly why I have perspective.'

'But you don't. Can't you see? Your mum was proud of you whatever you did. She actually thought you didn't have any faults,' Shell said, wide-eyed like nothing could be further from the truth. 'She died proud of you. That's much better than having two parents alive who will never accept you.'

'Of course it isn't!'

She got to her feet. 'You don't understand. I need to be around people that do.'

I watched her leave and sat alone and wet on the busiest street in London.

I wished I had no idea where she was going; unfortunately the answer seemed inevitable. I should have followed her but couldn't.

*

When things got like this, I usually phoned him. He just cheered me up, I suppose. He was self-employed (building, plumbing, bit of joinery) and so could knock off early if things were going slow. After a couple of messages we agreed to meet in a pub, which was not far away.

After ten minutes walking, I reached The Pig and Whistle. Inside there were no whistles or pigs, just a carpet speckled with the black remnants of chewing gum and walls discoloured by years of smoke, beer and sweat.

In the corner sat a man bashing the keys of his mobile phone, his bold green eyes entranced by the screen.

I went over to the oak-panelled booth and slipped onto the seat across from him. 'Slow down there Micky, there's steam coming off that thing.'

'Hold on, I've got to reply to this lassie.'

With a grand gesture he hit send and threw his phone down on the table. He smiled, a zap of positive energy fired straight from his soul. Micky hurried through life, not pausing or regretting, always wanting more, more, more. He was intelligent without being burdened by intellect; he

43

was permanently excited for no reason other than he was alive. He bounced to his own beat, a mind unaffected by reason, rationality or religion.

'How's tricks ma man?' he said.

As I write this, I realise how long it has been since I've seen Micky. But as I think about him I don't see him but hear his voice.

'Tell ye what, 'I've got some belting stories for ye.'

I'm not good with accents and I don't know what Micky sounded like to a native British person but to me his speech was harsh yet hopeful; colourful but matter-of-fact. I asked him once if all people from Scotland spoke like him. He muttered a few things that I didn't understand (probably insults) and asked if all people from Georgia asked such stupid questions.

In the pub that day he caught me stealing a glance at his left ear. 'What you looking at?' he said.

'An earring.'

'Aye. Diamond studded. Like it?'

'No.'

'I'm meeting this girl and she is,' he made an O with his thumb and middle finger and nodded. 'Plus the winning beard, skin heid combo.'

He had a number three hair cut and trimmed stubble the exact same length.

'Seems like a lot of effort.'

'I'm well into ma grooming nowadays. Women love it. You cannae show up with this type of quality unprepared. This is the Champions League my man.'

I glanced at the hand with which he clasped his pint. I didn't want to mention the cracked skin or the dirt under his nails. I don't think his new 'grooming' regime stretched that far.

He started to tell me how he met this date or perhaps it was how he met another girl. On he went, stopping only to interrupt himself, an endless loop of the same patter.

'Hoah!' He punched me dead on the arm. 'You're no listening to a word I say, are ye?'

I wasn't listening and it was so obvious that even Micky had noticed.

'What do you want to talk about then?' he said, deep inside one of his five-second bad moods. 'Your girlfriend?'

'Yes.'

He ran his finger across the scar under his left eye and sighed. 'What is it now?'

'I've just been at a meal with her parents and she lost it and walked out.'

'How?'

'No idea. Her parents are loaded and sent her to all the best schools and everything. They offered to buy her a house!'

'What's your point?'

'And she still hates them.'

'Maybes she doesnae want a hoose. Maybes she's she happy the one she's in. He took a gulp of his pint. 'Just because you've had it all doesnae mean that you get on with your parents. Same as if you've had nothing doesnae mean that yous don't get on.'

It was strange but I hadn't thought about it like that. I thought that everyone who had a better life than me and my mum should be happier. But some weren't.

That's when I should have realised that there was no real satisfaction in any house or school or job title or car if you weren't happy inside. And that might seem like

Spirituality Class 101 but it wasn't obvious to me back then.

'Shell has a new male friend. I think she's with him now.'

'Slow doon.' Micky's eyes shot back to me. 'She's just had a row with her Da and you've let her go off to be comforted by some other guy?'

'Is that an error?'

'Fatal. Now he's the go to guy when she's got a problem. Because you don't understand.'

'She actually said those words: that I don't understand and she needs to be with people who do.'

Micky made a clicking noise with his tongue. 'What's this guy like?'

'For a start his name is Sparky. What kind of a name is that?'

'I'd gee him a break on that one. You're called Zezva.'

'I know but not through choice. Anyway, it's not just his name. Everything about this guy is annoying. He lives in a mansion but thinks he is street because he says words like dude and craic. And even worse *he* lectures *me* about being some sort of upper class corporate whore.' I stopped and studied Micky's face. He looked amused. But then again he always did. 'What?'

'That look when you're raging.'

'What look?'

'It's always the same actions: one, nashers clacking away; two, eyes bulging out your nut; three, shouting your heid off. '

'One, I'm not denying because I don't know what you mean. Two, the same. Three, I'm not shouting.'

'Aye you are. Look even that old alky at the bar's

looking over. Last time he stopped staring at the barmaid's diddies was 1973.'

I leant in and lowered my voice, 'Actually, this Sparky guy is having a party. I need some back up if you want to come.'

Micky cracked his knuckles. 'You want to go round and gee him a doing?'

'Of course not.'

'Why did you say that you needed "back up" then?'

'I meant back up as in someone to talk to.'

'Oh right...' Micky picked his phone up and started scrolling through it. 'Anyhow, I'm a wee bit busy on –'

'They'll be loads of girls there.'

He looked up from the screen. 'Did you say he was rich?'

'Why?'

'If he is, that means all the women going will be minted too. Girls that went to paid school are always stunners.'

'They are?'

'Their parents didnae smoke or take a bevy when they were pregnant. Plus they made them wash and clean their teeth when they were weans.'

'Didn't your parents wash you and clean your teeth?'

'Listen son, if there was mouth wash around ma hoose, ma dad, would've drank it.' He smiled but it was differently from normal. 'Pint?'

We finished them and moved onto the next, starting the path to drunkenness. Each pint was less satisfying than the one before but each one I wanted more.

Clink, the glasses were collected. Bing, cried the fruit machine. Slosh, went the beer. Another hour passed. The afternoon eased into evening.

Micky pushed his empty glass away and buttoned up his jacket.

'Where are you going?'

'That date I telt you about,' he said.

'Can't you stay for a few more?' I said.

'Sorry, no can do.'

'One more?' I sounded pathetic even to my own ear.

He put his hand on my shoulder. 'Get yourself up the road, Zezva. Say sorry to Shell even if you arenae and pretend you understand even if you don't.'

He patted me on the back, turned and left the bar.

*

Buzz. No answer. I pressed the button again. Buzzzzz. Nothing.

I stepped back and shouted up at the flat, 'Shell... open up. I'm locked out.'

A light in the ground floor flat. A wrinkled hand drew back the curtain.

'Hello, Mrs Baxter. I can see you too. I spy with my little eye something beginning with Mrs B,' I said, smiling at the rapidly drawn curtains.

Patting myself down, I located my keys in my back pocket. I was sure I'd checked there. I let myself in and stumbled up the stairs to our door. I was drunk. Me and drink and Shell were a bad mix. I prayed she wasn't in.

Hearing a faint noise growing louder, I pressed my ear against the door.

A *GGGRRRLLL* sound regurgitated from the flat. It sounded like the hurls of impending death.

I sobered up. Fast.

I unlocked the door and burst inside. 'Shell? Where are

you?'

Looking. Left. Right. No lights in the kitchen or hall. Into the living room. The window open, wind billowing through the curtains.

I opened the cupboard, lifted a golf club out of the bag and stalked into the hall. A glow under the bathroom door. I tightened my grip and side-stepped towards the light.

I pushed the door open with my foot, drew the club above my right shoulder and waited for the door to creak open.

Shell lay on the floor: pale and semi-conscious. The smell of alcohol and sick filled the room.

I dropped the club, ran to her and crouched down. 'Are you OK?'

She didn't reply.

'Listen to me. What have you drank?' I said in the speed and tone I reserved for giving tourists directions to Buckingham Palace.

'Too many shots,' I translated from the slurred response.

'Shots? Who have you been doing shots with?'

'Sp -sp-arky.' She sat bolt upright. 'Is he here?'

'I hope not.'

'Need bed.'

'Are you going to be sick again?' I said, stroking her tangled hair.

She shook her head.

'You promise?'

She nodded her head.

She was certainly a lot sweeter when she was too imbibed to talk.

I lifted her and carried her into our bedroom. I lowered

her onto the mattress, lay her head on the pillow and pulled the duvet over her. She curled up into a ball.

I looked down at her and reflected on what a miserable bastard I was. I had a beautiful girlfriend, a good job and loyal friends like Micky. And all I did was moan. I'd driven her to this by my lack of compassion about the situation with her parents. I took a step back and gazed at her affectionately. A serene moment passed, as I enjoyed my new found perspective - before Shell was sick all over the bed.

DAY 4

I tried to sleep but the events of the night danced before my closed eyes. The fear when I entered the apartment. The body of Shell on the floor. The smell of vomit in my nose. The wretch of her stomach in my ears. Sick on the bed. Sick in the mind.

She squirmed next to me, her sleep deep yet troubled. Murmured whimpers from her lips. The poison decanting through her blood.

Sleep brought me no release as the terror of the night trapped me again.

Recently I'd become haunted by dark illusions. Neither asleep nor awake, my body was imprisoned in a semi-conscious torture night after night. Shadows fused with objects and morphed into deadly assassins. Wide awake in the depths of my sleep I could see them lurking; I could hear them under my bed; I could sense them outside the door. I rose to confront them but they weren't there. The demons of my psyche, always present but never found.

When the depths of the night passed, the light brought a touch of sleep, a fleeting moment before the rattle of the alarm began another day of buzzing fatigue.

So the days passed, filled with an energetic exhaustion; a soul that didn't rest, a mind that was never off-duty.

I thought I knew the cause but couldn't reach the pain.

It was nearly a year since my mother, Kekela, had left me. I remember the call, the numbness encircling my body, the relentless tears. She was killed in a car accident that she'd caused.

She died instantly; she felt nothing; she's at rest now, the doctors comforted - clichés of death, recounted by the living. The suddenness may have saved her pain but enhanced that of her bereaved son. Some say that drawn out deaths are the worst but at least people have some time. I only needed a second to say the words that had never left my mouth: I love you.

The month before she went, I watched a programme on TV. The protagonist was a blind person who miraculously regained their sight. At the end, a moment occurred when there were tears in your eyes and you realise that you are crying over a stranger brought into your life by a two-dimensional box of electricity. The cause was empathy, the recognition of how it must have felt for another human being, just like you, to go through such an experience. But the programme ends and the moment of compassion fades and all the promises of increased appreciation and changed perspective drift away and you become consumed with all your problems, those tiny irrelevancies, all over again.

After my mum was gone, I realised that I'd been blind. Her death opened a new wavelength of reality, stimulated by a melancholy that wouldn't fade. I told myself the feeling would go but all the things I didn't notice, and couldn't sense, that had previously left me untouched, reminded me of her. It wasn't birthdays and Mother's Days and things like that. It was more. When the sun set I knew I wouldn't see her when it rose. When the summer passed us by, I knew she wouldn't be there in the spring.

Give it time, they say.

And they are right. In a way. The sharpness of the hurt blunts into a constant regret; a trauma that touches you when you don't expect. As the days became months and then a year, time didn't heal but instead taught me to ignore the ache. And when it came to the surface I channelled the anger into the hatred of the father I'd never met. The dead and the living dead; I knew I wouldn't see either of them again.

That day, the torment was ended by the light of the dawn. I rose immediately, went into the kitchen and sat down at the table. There wasn't a sound except for the tick of the clock. Every second felt like a small death. But the black arrow didn't care and kept moving, as the face laughed at me and all my torment.

And in such times, I battle the want to think back to when my mum was alive and the clock didn't matter. But on it ticked, and as I sat still, time moved and moved it all a bit further away.

Further away from the Spring when I first came to London. Remembering the gown and square hat. The ceremony at 113 Chancery Court. A firm handshake from the President of the Law Society. My mum's yellow Marks and Spencer's suit. My Solicitor's Practicing Certificate framed on her wall.

A picture of a Georgian woman waving a Union Jack in front of Buckingham Palace. The lights of Leicester Square. The masses on Oxford Street. The strange of Soho. Getting lost on the Tube on the way back to my new house. Rehearsing my trip to work. Just in case Zezva. Just in case.

The first week. Presentations and introductions. White-teethed workers with shiny shoes. Bottomless bar tabs and free meals. Talk of client events on yachts in the South of France, casinos in Monte Carlo, hotels in Paris and New York. If you worked hard one day it could be you.

Two weeks in and I'd already received an invitation to the opening of an art gallery in Westminster. Fastening my bow tie. Slipping into my new dinner jacket – a present from my mum, tailored by a 'friend.' Looking in the mirror. I would make a good impression. It would be different this time. No one would laugh at Zezva Chichinadze anymore.

The expectant buzz in the gallery; the cocktail dresses and ball gowns, beiges and blacks, diamante tiaras and satin dresses. There were canapés, cocktails and caviar. And excitement. Excitement at being young, being rich and being there.

Noticing a group more familiar than the rest. They called me over. Handshakes and kisses on cheeks. They flocked around me, generous smiles and questions: how have your first weeks been? What department are you in? How many years qualified are you? Where did you train? On the questions went: questions about the topic of the night; about the man in the centre of the group; questions about me.

Until a man in a white dinner jacket approached. The conversation lulled and everyone waited. His name was Blackie. Shaking his hand. The hope and the illusion. And when I heard him speak the first crack appeared.

It was then that I learned there were two types in this way of life: the talkers and the listeners. The talkers decide who the listeners are. Listeners should smile and nod in the right place.

There were no more questions now, just Blackie's voice. Having no turn of phrase, wit or points of intrigue didn't stop him from monopolising every conversation. If anyone else spoke he'd instantly try to outdo them. If a listener had been ice-skating at the weekend: then Blackie would have been skating around the rings of Saturn. The competition had no winner – the losers were those listening.

Revelling in the attention, he launched into a joke. If a talker like Blackie tells a joke, a listener should laugh. If a newcomer in a burgundy tie and ill-fitting jacket doesn't laugh Blackie will say, 'Why aren't you laughing?'

The newcomer will usually mumble their apologies and feign amusement. Unless the newcomer is called Zezva. Then they will say, 'I didn't find it funny,' like a newcomer called Zezva did that night.

'Why don't you tell us a joke then if you're so hilarious.'

I don't know any jokes so I excused myself and hurried away.

Wherever you work there is always a Blackie and a Blackie above the Blackie. One day you have to stop running away from them. I hadn't reached that day yet.

As I stood and pretended to take in the artwork, I thought about how long was long enough before I should re-approach the group. I felt a tap on my arm. I turned to face a small, pretty girl with jet-black hair. She wore the white blouse and black skirt uniform of a waitress. She lowered her chin and raised her eyebrows like she expected me to say something. I was thirsty and a bit stressed so, 'Can I have a champagne, please?' was the obvious choice.

'Sorry none left,' she replied.

I looked at the fifteen or so glasses perched on the tray that she supported with her upturned right hand. 'What are they?'

'They are glasses of sparkling white wine imitating champagne to impress people like you.'

The dig wasn't very subtle but I still almost missed it. 'Who are people like me?'

'I doubt you know yourself.'

'Shouldn't you be serving the guests instead of insulting them?'

'I do what I want.' Her dark eyes smouldered but I didn't know what ignited them. 'What's your name then?'

'Zezva,'

'How dull.'

'Dull? No one has said that before.'

'Yeah well I'm not just anyone. My name's Shell since you ask.'

'Shell? Why's that a better name than Zezva?'

'It's a lot more natural.'

'More natural?'

'Stop repeating what I'm saying,' she said and punched my arm. It seemed a bit too firm to be playful. 'Why are you here anyway? Looking for a good investment?'

'I know that you hate repetition but remind me again why are you having a go at me?' I said, looking at this stranger who was almost standing on my toes, her bosom a couple of inches away from against my folded arms.

'I can tell you're a wannabe big shot swaggering round an art gallery.'

I decided to call her bluff, 'You're right I am a big shot.'

She looked me up and down. 'You could never be a big

shot. Not with that tux. It looks like you found it.'

'I did find it. On the rack of an expensive shop.'

She studied me and almost smiled. 'I like you. You're funny.'

I was sure I'd never been less likeable or amusing but she seemed drawn to that. I think this is where our problems started.

The conversation flowed, without the need for thought or reserve. We argued for over an hour. The conversation was edged. Every word felt like a challenge.

Then, following a particularly sharp bout of hostile flirting, she suggested that we should go for a walk. I agreed instantly. She took my hand, led me out the gallery, towards the Thames, along a path that changed my direction forever.

Down the South Bank we went. Stopping by the river. Two silhouettes in the cloudless night, our breath mingling in the air. Her face moved up towards mine. A rasp of breath, the firmness of her grip, the ferocity of the kiss. She stopped kissing me, grasped my hands, pushing them against my chest and propelled herself away. She walked backwards, not breaking eye contact.

'Where are you going?' I said.

'Home.'

'What about your job?'

'I was only helping out a friend.'

'You should go back.'

'You mean you don't want me to leave.'

I paused for a fragment of a second.

'I'll take that as a yes,' she said. 'Don't worry I'll give you my number.'

We messaged and agreed to meet in a bar called

Ricky's. She talked about the place like it was a landmark so I pretended that I'd been before. The problem was I'm not the type of guy who can just arrive at a first date. I need to know the place, what time to arrive, what to wear, who is going to be there, etc. Cool people can turn up and go with it. I can't.

The internet had no record of this Ricky's place and no one in my office had heard of it. Then I remembered someone who would definitely know. I scrolled through my phone until I found his number and rang it.

'Hello,' said a familiar voice.

'Hi. Is that Micky?'

'Aye. Who's that?'

'It's Zezva,'

'How did you get ma number?'

'You said to give you a call anytime I was down in London and I live here now.'

'Great but what are you calling for?'

I didn't understand his reaction – we'd got on so well when we played football together in Manchester. He'd moved down to England from Glasgow to live with a girl and stayed on after they'd broken up. He then moved to London. At the time, I didn't really know why he'd left. I was soon to find out.

'What's got into you?' I said.

'Has Terry put you up to this because I've telt him a million times I'm no paying him that money.'

'Who's Terry?'

'Big Terry fae the fitba team. Says we had a bet on a poker game. But we didnae. There wasnae any bet and if there was, it wasnae for as much as he's saying. Nae chance.'

'Micky I don't care if you owe Terry or anyone else any money. I just want to ask you if you know where a bar is.'

There was silence except for a few muffled breaths. 'Well, you never did get on with Terry that's a true. What bar is it?'

'It's called Ricky's. It's in the East End apparently. Have you heard of it?'

'Ricky's... Aye, I've been there.' He gave me directions before saying. 'I'm not being rude but it's no exactly your type of place...'

'Why?'

'It's a wee bit... doesnae matter.'

'A wee bit what? Cool for me?'

'Nah, that's every place.'

'Very funny. Right, I'll leave you to it.'

'You going already? That's pretty rude do you no think?'

'Micky, you made me feel about as welcome as herpes when you answered the phone and now you're getting annoyed at me for saying goodbye?'

'Nah you're brand new. I thought you were trying to trick us into paying Terry that ten grand.'

'You bet ten grand on a poker game?! You do know that dodgy bastard takes money off people for fun.'

'Could you no have telt me that before I had to leave Manchester?'

'Is that why you left? For the sake of ten grand. You pay that for a pint down here.'

'You're right on that one. But that guy was absolutely mental. He called in his hatchet men so I got out a there. Anyhow let's no talk about it.'

'Playing football down here?'

'Aye. Actually, now you mention it, I'm playing for a team down here and we need a right winger. If you fancy it? It's seven five pounds to lose, a hundred quid a draw, hundred and fifty for a win. You could definitely make the standard.'

I went for trials and did make the standard. At first I hung around with Micky at football. Then after football; then before football; then all the time. It's strange that I got back in contact with him trying to find out about the bar in which I was going to meet Shell. They were probably, in their own different ways, the reasons that I got through the next year.

I found Ricky's and the first date went well. It was strange because after that we didn't really continue to date or anything like that. We were almost together straight away. And when things started with Shell, they didn't stop. It was an infinite passion: incessant, indelible and ours. The more we argued, the more we made up. The more we made up, the more we argued. She moved into my flat six weeks after we met.

My life divided into two phases: having sex with Shell and thinking about having sex with her. Lust blurred my judgement: work was tolerable; her friends bearable.

I think at that time I felt like I was happy. In fact, I was happy. My mum was as well when she met Shell. I'd avoided introducing her to any of my past girlfriends because I knew of the over-reaction that would ensue.

'You're so kind putting up with my Zezva,' she said to Shell.

'You're so much nicer than my parents,' Shell told her.

'Now you both have me as a mother. I shall buy you a nice present for your house.'

'What'll it be?' Shell said, when she left. 'Something really fancy? My parents bought my brother Charlie a widescreen TV when he got his new flat.'

'Shell, you obviously don't know my mum. She wouldn't waste a month's pay on a big television. She hates TV.'

'She can't hate TV.'

'She does. We didn't have one when I was growing up.'

'Why?'

'In case I picked up some bad language or it interrupted my four hours of homework.'

My mum returned two hours later with a white woolly rug. I still remember the sincerity with which she laid it down on the floor. Shell looked disappointed and didn't say thank you. My mum didn't notice. I did.

As our relationship neared the year mark our infatuation began to fade. The circle of sex and arguments became a spiral of arguments and further disagreements. Then the clashes stopped.

The phone call on September 14. The drive to Norwich. The hospital. The morgue. Her cold milky face. The black of the funeral. My mother's body in a chestnut casket, the red cross of Georgia and England on top.

Fifteen people gathered. Some faces I didn't know. Black clothes for the women from the Black Sea. Shell fidgeting in the background. A minister talking regretfully about a woman he hadn't met. The coffin lowered into the grave. Clay soil thudded off its top. The woman who could never settle resting forever.

I shook the minister's hand and that of her latest man; Michael, I think he was called. Two months in a relationship that wouldn't have lasted. The mourners shuffled home. Sitting in the car, I didn't feel sad because it couldn't have happened. She couldn't be there in the ground. I would see her again.

A letter from an adult to a red-faced man of my youth. Written carefully in Georgian and sent first class. Then a reply.

> *This family has always been well thought of within this town. Kekela brought disgrace upon us all. She died the moment she had a child out of wedlock and then left this house. Please do not write again.*

The saddest letter I've read. And at that moment, I was glad she was dead so she couldn't read his words and all those bitter, selfish, deluded people couldn't harm her ever again.

I wrote back,

> *Dear Granddad,*
>
> *My mother may have had a child from wedlock but at least she died knowing she gave everything to her child. You will die knowing you gave nothing to your child but misery. It is you that have let your family down not my mum. You should not take pride from this but shame.*
>
> *Yours sincerely,*
>
> *Zezva*

I put it in an envelope, stamped and addressed it. But I didn't post it. I don't know why. Maybe I couldn't push my remaining family away – even though they were strangers to me. So I lay the letter in a box under my bed.

I made sure as few people found out about my mum as possible, especially at work. Those that knew didn't know how to act around me. There is no conversation stopper like someone recently bereaved. People swung from being over-sombre to trying to show they were not going to be over-sombre.

Where some cowered and others squirmed, Micky took it upon himself to make everything all right, helping in the only way he knew how. More golf, more football, more nights out, more talking, more ideas of 'lads' holidays. He did little things to make a difference, like phoning me every day to tell me about himself rather than every second day.

The one who knew least how to cope was Shell. Unsure what to say or do, she'd hurry out my way, finding excuses to be out of the house.

And as I sat at that kitchen table, on that dank Saturday morning, almost a year after my mum's death, I realised that all I had left was a stupid name, a job I didn't want and a girlfriend who I sometimes thought hated me.

*

A faint creak punctured the silence. A draught hit the back of my neck. I turned to face the gradually opening door. Through its breach crept Shell.

She closed the door in the most deliberate of fashions, walked across the room in the manner of someone who knew that they were being watched, and slipped into the chair across from me. I looked past her at the condensation weeping down the window panes.

'Did you sleep well?' she said.

'Yes very well,' I said, unable to remember what sleeping well felt like.

'What are you doing today?'

She'd only asked two questions and I was already tired

of her attempts to avoid the topic, so I just came right out with it, 'What happened last night?'

'I drank too much.'

'I'm aware of that.'

'Are you not going to shout at me?'

'You look disappointed.'

'I know you're annoyed. Let's get it over with now.'

'OK then let's get it all over.' I leant towards her. 'All of it.'

'What's all of it?'

'Us. It didn't used to be like this......'

She chewed on her scarlet- painted fingers nails and then lowered her hand. 'We have such different lifestyles and outlooks. At the start our differences were fun. Everyone else I went out with agreed with everything I said, whether I was right or wrong.'

'Probably wrong,' I said.

'See that's what I loved,' she said, pertinently speaking in the past tense. 'You challenged me. But it doesn't work anymore.'

'What has changed?'

She lifted her eyes to meet mine. 'We're not suited to each other, are we?'

'We've been together for almost two years. We must be... in some way.'

'To tell the truth I was having doubts before everything happened with your mum.'

'So basically you've stayed with me because you feel sorry for me?'

She paused. It wasn't long; it was significant. 'I know this year has been hard for you but it's not been easy for me either. I guess I felt trapped.'

'You're never here. If I'm trapping you I'm not doing a very good job.'

'I'm not saying you forced me to go out with you or anything. I'm saying, you know...' She put her hand on her forehead and rubbed like she was trying to scratch an invisible itch. 'Maybe we should just end it.'

'No!' I snapped before I'd even thought about what she'd said. 'Definitely not.'

'You know it's not working.'

I did. But I thought that I wouldn't work if I was alone. 'We can't just give in. Now this year is over perhaps it'll get better.'

'Well, perhaps if you showed an interest in one, my beliefs; two, my life's work; three, the struggle then we wouldn't need to find something in common,' she said, confirming my worst fears. It had got to the stage where we needed to manufacture a connection.

'I know,' she reached over the table and clasped my forearm. 'Come to the protest.'

'What protest?'

'The one we're all going to on Wednesday.'

'I'm working. You know that.'

'Phone in sick. Do it. Please, please, please, please...' she said, tugging my arm with every beg.

'I can't afford to lose that job.'

'What do you prefer - me or your work?' she said. I paused to contemplate what was quite a tricky question: it was like being asked whether I preferred a kick in the balls or a punch in the face. Both made me miserable but in different ways. The plus sides of each were that work paid me whereas Shell had sex with me. Recently these had both been monthly transactions so were hard to separate.

'I can't believe you're actually thinking about that question,' she said, letting go of my arm.

'I wasn't thinking about it.'

'Yes, you were. You're always moaning about your job as well.'

'I know. Come here.' She lifted her hand from the table, avoiding my attempt to take it. 'Come on Shell. I'm sorry.'

'How sorry?'

I tried to smile. 'So sorry that I'll come to the protest.'

'Are you serious?'

To my own surprise I nodded.

'Yes, wooooo!' She got up from her seat and sat on my knee and hugged me with all her force. I drew back and saw the past flickering in her eyes, the girl I once adored, who I thought was going to change my life, staring back at me for the final time.

*

Despite our earlier moment, as usual Shell and I had different plans on the Saturday night. Shell said she was going out with her friends. I didn't have the energy to ask if Sparky would be there. Or I didn't want to know the answer more like. On the other hand, I openly told her I was meeting Liz and she openly didn't care. In a way, she seemed to encourage my friendship with Liz. I asked her once if she was jealous and she laughed and said something like, 'As if someone like Liz would go out with you.' I got defensive and argued that she would.

Thinking back, arguing with my girlfriend about if another girl would go out with me was a bit weird but I suppose that's what me and Shell were like.

*

I walked over the bridge with the Dog running ahead of me and towards the bandstand. The morning rain had long cleared and evening sun was out and people were lying on the grass and listening to a jazz band. Liz was standing on the edge of the lawn wearing a cream top and slim-fitting jeans.

She saw me, did a little skip as she approached and gave me a hug. She released me and said, 'How are you?' She spoke in a Cornish accent, which was nice and soft. I'd never known anyone from Cornwall before her but I thought it must be a nice place and I should visit one day.

'I'm fine,' I said, crouching down and re-attaching the Dog's lead.

'Who's this lovely thing?'

'We're looking after him for Shell's friend, Sparky.'

'Why?'

'Because he damages furniture and ours is a lot cheaper than his.'

'That's not true! He doesn't look like he could damage anything. What's he called?'

'The Dog.'

'Zezva,' she said, slapping my arm. 'What's he really called?'

'The Dog.'

'He's not.'

'Alright anything you want then. Come on, let's walk.'

'You're so stroppy!' she said and laughed like it was a good thing. She used to laugh at a lot of things I did that other people found annoying.

When Liz and I met we didn't sit in a bar or have a coffee or anything like that. We walked around and talked.

As usual she did most of the talking. That day she talked about her sister's husband and something that happened at a wedding.

The route was pre-determined by tradition: from the bandstand to Avenue Gardens through symmetrical lines of roses: orange, blue, white, burgundy and red.

'You're not listening, are you?' came to my ears.

'No,' I conceded.

'Typical.' She scowled at me but I could see she was suppressing a smile. 'Well, I'm not happy with you.'

'If you're not happy at someone you shouldn't smile at them.'

'You're the expert Zezva...'

'I won't ask what that means.'

'It must be because I'm blonde. No one takes me seriously.'

'Who doesn't take you seriously?'

She breathed in through her nose and laughed again but this time nervously. 'Everyone.'

'That can't be true.'

'It is. Like at the hospital,' she said, talking about her job as a radiographer. 'They're amazed when I do anything correctly. One of the consultants actually patted me on the head like a dog the other day.'

'Patted you on the head?'

'Yes, I think it's because I'm small. People do it all the time.'

'You aren't small. And I've told you about this before,' I took a sharp intake of breath and could feel my fingers twitching. 'I mean for God's sake stand up for yourself more. You can't let people walk all over you.'

'Zezva... you're shouting,' she said, nodding towards a

couple sitting on a bench about thirty metres away.

'Just because they're nosey doesn't mean I'm shouting.'

'You're still shouting,' she said in a soft voice. She stopped walking and studied me with those turquoise eyes, kaleidoscopes of greens and blues; eyes that were never the same to look at twice. 'Let's sit down,' she said, pointing to a bench.

'OK, but not there. I don't want those people listening in.'

We walked on for a bit and sat down on another bench. Liz swallowed quite deliberately and looked at me sternly and I could see what was coming. 'Zezva, don't take this the wrong way but are you OK?'

'Yes,' I said because I was.

'Don't be defensive.'

I didn't see how the word *yes* was proof of defensiveness but I didn't say that in case I got accused of being defensive again. 'Everything's fine.'

'It's not though, is it? You're twitchy and all agitated. I thought it was getting better.'

'I'm fine,' I repeated, subtly trying to relax the muscles in my face. We were sat in Queen Mary's garden surrounded by tropical plants, giant ferns and sunflowers. I pretended to study them with my new relaxed face.

'Come on what's wrong?' she said.

She really wasn't letting this go. 'You tell me if you're such an expert,' I said.

She opened her mouth to reply but ended up gawping with her full lips and looking a bit like a fish.

'Just say it,' I said.

'Say what?'

'That I've not been the same since my mum.'

69

'You haven't.'

'The one reason I like spending time with you is because you don't sit me down on benches and make me have conversations like this.'

'That's the one reason you like spending time with me?'

'No, of cou–'

'Because I don't challenge you basically,' her right leg swung over her left and her whole body faced away from me.

I didn't know what to say. I mean, what was I meant to do? Start listing all the reasons I did like spending time with her? Then I thought actually I will do that but she was still looking away and the moment had kind of passed.

The Dog lay on his back under the bench, exposing his chest to the egg yolk sun that was slipping below the horizon. The outlines of the swallows and the thrushes soared across the lavender clouds.

I stole a glance at Liz. Her face was coloured peach, the freckles on her nose barely visible in the softening light.

I sat there and took in the scene and thought it would have been beautiful if I hadn't ruined it.

*

It was dark when we got up from the bench. We wound through the floodlit flowerbeds to Broadwalk, the canopy of trees blackening the great boulevard. The Dog zipped in figures of eight between our bodies, barking excitedly. At the edge of the park, we passed the entrance to London Zoo, the shrieks of the chimpanzees filling the air. We reached the canal boat, ducked under the roof and slipped onto the wooden benches. The engine started and we slid away.

Ten minutes later, the bargeman lassoed the rope over a post, leapt off and secured the mooring to the jetty. We clambered out and cut through the outdoor market to the main road, the railway bridge announcing Camden Lock. The lights of the closed shops lit the pavement; their windows displaying headless manikins dressed in bondage gear. A man handed out flyers for the all-night tattoo parlours; he didn't waste one on us.

'How square must we look?' Liz said. It felt like a long time since she'd spoken. 'He didn't even think about giving us a flyer.'

'He could probably see I was about to faint at the thought of it.'

'Not another phobia! Don't tell me you're frightened of needles as well?'

'Of course I am. I'm scared of anything sharp,' I said. That made her smile. I felt like I'd won her back a bit at that point. Typical it was just as we stopped by the entrance of the Tube Station.

'Are you playing tomorrow?' she said.

I played football for the same team as her boyfriend, Matty. That is how I'd met her. 'Yes,' I said. 'Is Matty?'

'I guess so,' she said, which was a strange response because she knew that he was. But I'd asked the question and I knew he was as well.

'Have you done anything nice with Shell this weekend?' Liz said. It felt like a retort.

'We don't have that much in common.'

'You must have something in common you've been going out for twenty two months.'

'To be precise.'

Her features stiffened. 'OK, Zezva...'

71

'What?'

'Nothing... I better go.' She stood on her tip toes, brushed her lips against my cheek, turned and went into the station.

DAY 5

The feel of the black leather. The aroma of the polish. Gleaming boots nestled beneath my crisp new kit. The smell of freshly sheared turf. The sound of the ball hitting the net. The first day of the football season. A new start. Another page.

I walked between the parked cars with my kit bag slung over my shoulder, feeling awake for the first time in weeks. Continuing towards the clubhouse, I saw a new sign erected above the main entrance:

Haverton Rovers, Your Local Club, Est. 1902

I peered through the window into the clubhouse at the regulars enjoying a pre-match drink. I waved in response to their cheered salute and headed towards the changing area. The boys were congregated outside the entrance. Some were clustered around a pile of bags lumped on the floor; others formed a splinter group trying various tricks and flicks with a ball. A glorious scene of male bonding replicated in car parks up and down the country.

Handshakes, nods and back-slaps. It seemed like yesterday that we were celebrating our promotion, and here we were, in August, ready for our first league game.

'Look here he is,' Matty said, squinting at me through his piggy eyes. A scar cracked across his stone-like face, running from forehead to the crag of his nose. Mean of spirit and lumbering in grace, he made an ideal centre-half. When he wasn't bullying strikers on the pitch he was picking on me off it. 'I was just talking bout you, Zezva. I heard you had a missus but you know what I thought? That can't be true. As if he could ever get a bird. But then I seen you both, dint I?'

The other players laughed. Half of the noise was relief he wasn't picking on one of them.

'It's the truth. I was there. His missus is one of those soap dodging hippies, int she? She's munting, mate,' Johnny joined in. Whenever Matty was on the attack, Johnny would slip out of his shadow, gnashing his buck teeth in sycophantic support. If Matty was a punch in the face, Johnny was a constant flick in the ear; not as painful but ultimately as irritating. Evidently, the laugh that his comment had received had filled Johnny with courage. He rubbed his blonde curly hair, his goggly eyes springing out from his face, 'I'd rather shaft a prozza than her.'

'She probably is one. Zezva's her only punter,' Matty said, unwilling to be outdone by his sidekick.

They looked at me waiting for my response but they weren't going to get one. I'd heard it all before about Shell and I certainly didn't care what they thought about her. It was like two monkeys throwing rocks at you in the zoo; you wished it wouldn't happen but with such low forms of intelligence you couldn't take it personally.

Ignoring them, I turned to the unusually quiet Micky. He was staring straight ahead, his mouth open catching flies. Following his gaze, I saw Liz coming towards us. She was wearing a fitted top coat that matched her sienna brown ankle boots. The wind had ruffled her blonde hair, which was usually parted down the middle and straight. She smiled in my direction but continued past me to Matty. In a flash his hand was around her waist.

'Hello,' she said, greeting the group.

'Hi,' murmured the now bashful crowd.

'I could hear you laughing round the corner,' she said. 'What were you talking about?'

'Just how ugly Zezva and his bit of fluff are,' Johnny said, like a child trying to impress the best looking girl in the playground.

'Jonathan, stop it. Zezva's very good looking,' Liz said.

'No one was asking your opinion, sweetheart. Why don't you toddle off to the bar and get yourself a drink,' Matty said, clearly reeling from the good-looking comment.

'You toddle off to the bar,' she retorted.

He took her by the arm and led her away from the group. After an animated exchange Liz did toddle off towards the bar.

'That told her,' said Johnny on Matty's return.

'It's called having a firm hand,' Matty said, cracking a smile.

'How did you get her anyhow?' Micky said. 'She must be like a hundred times better looking than you. Are yous even the same species?'

Matty laughed. In the team Micky and Micky alone was allowed to speak to him in such a way.

'Do you think he date rapes her every time they go out?,' Johnny said, always on the side of the latest winner.

Whack, Matty clipped Johnny on the back of the head. 'Don't get cheeky, sunshine.' With that they both loped off to get changed, Johnny murmuring his apologies on the way.

I watched them go and thought about the way Matty had spoken to Liz and how aggressive it had looked and wondered if I'd been the same when I shouted at her in the park the night before and if the old couple had looked at me like I looked at Matty and if I was as bad as him.

'What are you thinking about?' Micky said.

'Liz.'

'I know. Me too. She is amazing, isn't she? That butter wouldnae melt thing combined with that face and her wee —'

'I wasn't thinking about her like that.'

'Nah, me neither,' Micky said, staring at the clubhouse door where Liz had just entered. 'I wasnae joking neither when I said they things to Matty. I mean, what does she see in him?'

I shrugged. They were truly the oddest couple I knew. Except me and Shell perhaps.

'It must be looks,' Micky said.

'I doubt that.'

'Of course it's looks. He has looks. Ugly ones but he has them. He has *no* personality.'

'So how does that work?'

'If he doesnae have a personality then it must be his looks because he has them on his face like a nose and eyes and stuff,' Micky screwed up his features like he was annoyed at having to explain such basic things to me.

I picked up my bag and followed him towards the changing room still not sure what he was going on about. The world really was simple to Micky. But then again he only had one outlook to consider: his own.

*

76

The turf was firm beneath our studs as we jogged a warm up lap. A decent crowd of roughly five hundred people gathered in our one stand. A new season but the same faces. They stamped their feet and cheered as we ran past. The father of the club, George, was there, rigidly clapping his hands, wheezing the most vociferous encouragement he could muster. George had played for and watched the club for over sixty years. He could often be found in the club bar holding court on the club's glory days. Even Matty treated George with some degree of reverence.

George's wife, Ethel, was another ever-present yet seemed to stand further away from her husband with each game. I once asked her why. 'He's boring,' she said, enunciating her words with as much bitterness as her false teeth would allow. As well as an excuse to ignore her life-long companion, Ethel attended the games to provide tactical advice in the bar afterwards. You weren't truly part of the team until you'd been 'Etheled.' She once chastised me for my defensive skills. 'You need to sniff the danger,' she said, snorting and pointing at her nose. 'Sniff it.'

For some reason I started copying her and sniffing the air too. 'What does the danger smell like?'

'Death.'

'Death?'

'That's what you need to learn.'

'What do I do then?'

'React quicker. Much quicker. You're too slow,' she said, delivering the prognosis with a hand rested on her prosthetic hip.

We completed our circuit of the pitch and began to perform various stretching exercises. Tiring of the ritual, I noticed Liz on the touchline and went over to say hello. Since she'd arrived she'd put on our club's woolly hat and matching scarf.

'Why are you dressed like that? It's summer.'

'It's cold,' she said, crossing her arms and hugging herself to prove the point. 'I really should have better things to do than to watch this.'

As the conversation went on her laugh seemed to grow louder, drawing the attention of Matty, who was now *coincidentally* jogging past. He greeted Liz with a tap on the bum before kissing her cheek. He looked at me, a proud grin spreading across his face.

'Matty, stop it,' Liz said.

'You weren't saying that last night,' he said. He winked at me and jogged on.

Liz waited until he left and said, 'We didn't do anything like that, don't listen to him.'

'It's none of my business if you did.'

'I know,' she said. 'It's just that... it doesn't matter.'

She re-arranged her hat and pulled her gloves up and did this strange kind of hum whilst she did it. She was obviously still embarrassed by Matty's comment, which was making me embarrassed, so I mumbled something and went back to the group.

As we did the pre-match stretches, the clouds seemed to close in, colouring the pitch a dark green. I finished my quad stretch and looked up to see Matty stood in front of me. He tugged at his balls and jutted out his jaw. 'You think I don't know you was with Liz last night.'

'All we were doing was walking in a park.'

'I don't care if you was skipping around a fucking monastery, mate. It ain't happening again.'

'She can decide that not you.'

My teammates stopped their stretching and gazed at me with nervous confusion, their minds distrusting what their ears had heard. Had *Zezva* really said that to *Matty*?

The only person not caught off guard was Matty. The words had barely left my mouth and he was advancing towards me. He had his fighting walk on: arms spread, fists clenched, feet splayed outwards; a gait that said 'BRING IT ON.' He began our debate with an open handed push that quarried into the centre of my chest. As I fought to regain my breath, he put his hand on the back of my head with menacing gentleness. His hiss was slow and clear, 'No, I decide who speaks to my missus.'

'Get out my face,' I wheezed.

He somehow managed to move even closer, the bones of his skull digging into my forehead. 'What you gonna do if I don't? You fucking ponce.'

His warm spit hit my face. 'I'm going to do this,' I said and pushed him away.

He stepped back. His eyes seemed to withdraw into his cranium, shaded by the knit of his mono-brow. He lifted his hand and cocked his wrecking-ball fist. A moment to make a decision. Stand there and permanently blemish my face or run and eternally scar my dignity. Fortunately the decision was made for me as our Gaffer stepped in between us.

'You two cut it out or you'll both be on the bench,' he said before turning to me. 'Zezva, why do you always need to cause problems?'

'He started it.'

'Stop being a baby, Zezva. Does it look like I care who started it?' the Gaffer said, his six foot five frame towering over me. 'Leave his girl alone and concentrate on playing football.'

'Leave her alone? I went for a walk in the park with her. I didn't attack her.'

'It's his girl. If he don't want you playing on the swings with her, you don't. And you don't bring it into the team neither.'

I looked around at my teammates for support. The majority looked at the floor, embarrassed at the scene I was subjecting them to. Their reaction corroded any will I had left to continue the confrontation. Overwhelmed and over-matched, another small injustice to add to the list, I walked away. As I left an exhalation of smirks and the words of the Gaffer followed my path. 'Zezva, you can start on bench. If you want to know why, it's for damaging team spirit.'

I reached the bench and sat down. I watched Micky jogging to me. 'What has got into you?'

'What has got into me? He started on me for doing nothing and I'm in the wrong?'

Micky rested his hand on my shoulder, 'Have you no worked it out yet? With boys like Matty doesnae matter if you're in the right or wrong... you're always in the wrong.'

'No, you're not.'

Micky opened his eyes really wide and pressed his finger against his temple and twisted it. 'Aye, you are.'

*

I sat on the bench alone, the wind blowing rain into my face. The other substitutes shuffled around the dugout, giving each other the full opportunity of being the one who had to sit next to me. A new guy called Dave or something broke rank and sat down and the rest used him as a sort of human shield and crammed in next to him.

When the match kicked off, calm descended as my love of the game took over and in my imagination I was kicking and heading every ball.

The evenly-matched game was edged by the obvious disregard both teams had for each other. Despite both teams creating a number of chances, the contest was still goalless at half-time.

When the whistle blew I was no longer distracted by the football and my mind stilled. The players trudging off were no longer brave teammates fighting a brutal opposition and an unjust referee but the traitors who refused to back me up. The other substitutes walked towards the changing room but I didn't follow. Instead I huddled in the corner of the concrete dug out and pulled up my training top hood to shield myself from the elements.

'Sleeping are you, son?' said a voice that bore a weary rasp. Under the brim of my hood I saw George holding onto his hat, his tweed trousers flapping in the wind.

I yanked down my hood and sat upright. 'No, just thinking over a few things, Mr Wilson.'

'Why are you not playing?' he said, the wrinkles that surrounded his hazel eyes contracting with concern. 'I thought you'd be the first player picked.'

'I think it's tactical,' I lied.

'Aye, maybe it's for the best my boy. It's a horrible day this. It reminds me of the second round of the FA Cup back in '64. We used to qualify for it regular back then. I doubt we'll see the day again. Well, I won't anyway.' For a moment he seemed to gaze beyond me at his nearing morality.

'You never know,' I said. He looked at me regretfully. We both knew.

'Best get back,' George said, as a cheer rose from the crowd, marking the players' return to the pitch. He turned and hobbled away, nodding acknowledgement to the Gaffer who strode past him towards me. He moved like a man who had something to say. 'Why didn't you come in at half-time?'

I shrugged in a deliberately casual manner.

'You're not playing today, Zezva. Your behaviour has been a disgrace. I'll speak to the committee and your match fee will be revoked too.'

'I'll adjust my budget accordingly,' I said, staring ahead at the rain lashing onto the pitch.

He turned his back on me and didn't reply. Despite him sitting at the opposite end of the bench to me, I could feel his seething presence as the second half kicked off. By now the ground resembled a quagmire and all poise went out of the game. The tumultuous affair was epitomised by the crunching tackle that led to our right-midfielder, Nico, suffering a suspected broken ankle. Carried off on a stretcher Nico writhed in pain as he passed the bench. We patted him, offering consolation that we knew he probably couldn't take in.

Not one for sentiment, the Gaffer appeared more concerned about Nico's replacement than his wellbeing. Turning to look at the substitutes, he massaged the bristles of his moustache. In front of him sat a striker, two defenders, a goalkeeper and me, the regular right-midfielder, the player of the year and the person Nico had replaced in the starting line-up. The Gaffer was in the unenviable position of either going back on his word to not bring me on or appearing to be stubborn and affecting the team's chances of winning.

'Zezva, strip-down you're on,' he said. I couldn't believe an authoritarian such as the Gaffer had gone back on his disciplinary edict; he must be facing extreme pressure from the committee to perform well this season.

I took my tracksuit off and a moment later, dazed by the unexpected turn of events, I was running onto the pitch. Exposed from the shelter of the dugout, each drop of rain felt like a nail hammering into my body. Instantly sodden, my shirt became plastered to my torso.

Lacking a proper warm up, I found it difficult to adapt to the pace of the game. My touch was heavy, I was weak on the ball, my decision making poor. My teammates' initial encouragement turned into criticism as their frustration built.

With twenty minutes left I found myself with space on the wing. I received a drilled pass into my feet from Micky. I took a good first touch and avoided a tackle with a neat flick. I saw some space to attack and dribbled through the opening. I beat the last defender and found myself one on one with the goalkeeper. I raised my leg to stroke the ball into the net when I felt a cynical clip of my heels that sent me crashing down into the mud. Mired in the sludge, I waited to hear the whistle signifying the award of a penalty. I rolled over to see the referee running away, his hand outstretched signalling to play on; a swarm of remonstrating players following him. Now on my knees, arms sprawled out incredulously, an opposition player leant down and barked in a London drawl, 'On yer feet yer fuckin cheat.'

And on my feet I was. I took a step to him and swung my fist. My knuckles hit his cheek, a crisp thwack singing above the howling breeze. More assailants were coming now, wearing the same coloured shirts and furious expressions. I faced my enemies at last. They were the people at work, Sparky, Matty, the kids who laughed at me in school, the man who crashed into my mum, that old Georgian bastard who disowned us. I could see their fists connecting with my body but I could feel no pain. I returned each blow with a vengeance, swinging at anyone in sight.

Dragged away from the melee, I saw all of the other players were concentrated in one area of the pitch jostling, grappling and pushing. Before I could compose myself the referee approached. His hand triggered upwards, a red card in the grey sky.

I walked past the opposition players towards the touchline. They were visibly furious yet didn't dare to step closer. I'd never experienced anyone being scared of me before. To be honest, I liked it.

After I left the pitch, the first person I saw was George. He certainly wouldn't be reminiscing in years to come about the time that Zezva Chichinadze sparked a twenty two man brawl.

Nearing the clubhouse, I passed Ethel. She stared through me at the pitch; a snub that stung more than a hundred of her scathing words.

Finally there was Liz at the very end of the dilapidated stand. I looked away as I passed. I couldn't bring myself to witness her reaction.

I hurried towards the sanctity of the clubhouse trying to blink away the throbbing pain in my eye. As I opened the door, I heard a curdling cry of joy. I didn't need to turn around to know the opposition had scored or that it was my fault.

*

The patter of my studs on the cement floor was the only sound in the changing area. It was strange to be alone in a place that was usually packed with people - like that strange feeling of going to a night club in the day time to pick up the jacket you drunkenly left the night before.

I showered quickly, trying to leave before my teammates got back. I was almost dressed when they filed into the changing room: soaked and shattered, mud dripping from their bodies. They sagged onto the benches each one lost in his own thoughts. The Gaffer came in last and stood in the middle of the room looking down upon his defeated warriors.

'Boys, you were superb out there. Great battling, great commitment, you fought from the first minute until the last. The supporters that stood out in those conditions couldn't have asked for any more.' His voice was becoming louder with each word. 'Playing them with eleven let alone ten is hard enough. But we won't discuss that now.'

One by one the players set their eyes upon the person who had lost them the game, their bonus money and peace of mind for the rest of the weekend.

'Zezva, you must be as thick as pig shit. You knew they were gonna to try to get yer sent off and you fell for it you mug,' said Matty - a man who had done a six month stretch for GBH giving anger management advice.

'He was too busy thinking about your missus to

concentrate on the game,' said Johnny, buying the first ticket to the band wagon.

'Too fucking right,' Matty said, pointing a stubby finger towards me.

'Worst punch I've ever seen, an all. Hit him with your handbag did yer?' Johnny said, safely fortressed between Matty and the wall.

I pulled on my jumper and was fully dressed. I smoothed down my clothes, rolled up my sleeves and took four paces over to the corner that seated Matt and Johnny. I stood over them and said, 'If you stand up I'll punch you.'

Neither of them moved.

'Come on then,' I said. 'Stand up.'

They just sat there. Matty entered most confrontations assured that the other person would back down first. Maybe looking at me that day he couldn't be so sure.

'Zezva, leave this instant' the Gaffer yelled. 'You're in big trouble for your behaviour today.'

I walked backwards out of the room, my eyes not leaving Matty or Johnny sat on the bench.

*

I wandered through the streets, thinking about my anger, frightening in its brevity; sorrowing in its veracity. Fire burning through my control and branding my reputation. And when the heat cooled, it was replaced by a composed hatred; the urge to inflict pain upon Matty, whilst wishing he'd return a greater hurt upon me.

Headlights shimmered in the puddles. An engine revved faintly behind. A car pulled up beside me. The passenger door opened. Inside sat Liz.

'Get in, you're soaking,' she called out. Matty's warning repeated in my head, *Stay away from her.*

'I can't,' I said.

'Don't be ridiculous, you can't walk home in this weather.'

'I'm fine.'

She leant across the passenger seat, her eyes dragging me inside. 'Please.'

Swaying in procrastination, I glanced up and down the street. It was deserted. I quickly got inside the car feeling both reluctance and relief.

The first thing I said to Liz was, 'Sorry,' - and they say I'm not properly English.

'Why?'

'You know why... the fight.'

'I haven't seen you like that before.'

When she said that I realised that I didn't regret punching that guy; I regretted punching the guy in front of Liz. I don't know what that said about me.

'Was it,' she lowered her voice, 'the argument with Matty at the start?'

'No, nothing to do with that.'

'Why were you arguing with him?'

'Tactics... like who was playing where.'

Her hand met my jaw and guided my face towards the driver's seat. I met her eyes. 'Don't listen to him, Zezva.'

'What? About the tactics?'

'Yes. About the tactics...' she let it hang and I thought that maybe she wasn't talking about the tactics but wasn't sure. 'Come on. I'll take you somewhere nice.'

*

A black awning billowed in the wind. Above, a sign

announced in golden writing:

Annie's Tea and Biscuit Room

We splashed through the puddles towards the glow of the interior. Inside, we sat in the far corner next to the window. The seats were straw matted; the tables covered with blue-chequered cloths. Behind the wooden counter, a large brass AGA hissed steam round the kitchen.

'It's nice isn't it?' Liz said.

'Yes, I suppose it is.'

'I knew this would cheer you up.'

A waitress came over, pulled a pencil out of her apron and tapped it against a notepad. 'Hello, Liz. You haven't been in here for a while.'

'I was here on Tuesday morning.'

'So you were my dear. I'm getting forgetful in my old age,' she said, the capillaries in her cheeks accentuated as she smiled. 'Is this nice looking man your boyfriend?'

Liz's face blotched up and she shook her head but didn't actually say no.

'Oh I'm sorry,' the waitress said.

'Don't worry. Can we have two scones and two teas, please?' Liz said.

'Of course, my darling,' the waitress said. She picked up the menus, touched Liz on the shoulder and left. She either genuinely liked Liz or was pulling out all the stops to get a good tip.

'How does she know you so well?'

'I came in with my mum and dad and they asked loads of questions so she's never forgotten me.'

'Why did they ask loads of questions?'

'My family are very fond of old tea rooms. It's a hobby of my parents. We used to visit them when I was younger.'

I burst out laughing. 'Your parents have a hobby of visiting tea rooms?'

'Yes! It's a nice hobby. What did you used to visit when you were younger then?'

'We used to visit a lot of men's houses.'

'I'm sure you exaggerate your childhood.'

'I don't.'

'Your upbringing explains a lot about you.'

'And yours too? Miss Cup of Tea.'

'My family are very normal, thank you. We stayed in the same house in Cornwall and my Gran and Granddad would come to visit all the time and all the rest of the family were really close and everything.'

'Everyone thinks their lives are normal when they're kids. It's because you don't know anything else.'

The waitress returned and placed a Royal Doulton teapot and two matching cups and saucers on the table.

Liz poured her tea and said, 'Is it true you could have been a professional footballer but your mum wouldn't let you?'

'Maybe if we hadn't moved around so much.'

'Was it your dream?'

'I like playing but I don't think I could spend every day around people like...'

'Like who?'

'No one.'

'Matty?'

I poured myself a cup of tea out of the pot, added milk and sugar and slowly stirred. 'What about you - what was your dream?'

'Nice change of subject... ballet dancing. I went to the Royal Academy of... you're laughing.'

'I can't help it. I'm predisposed to laugh at things like orchestras, novels and ballet dancing. Being a philistine was a useful survival technique when I was growing up.'

'Make your mind up. A minute ago you were saying you're too sophisticated for football players, now you're laughing at ballet.' Her eyes opened wider and she said, 'In fact, that's your problem. You don't know what you are or what you believe.'

As I said before I didn't like to get angry in front of Liz but it really wound me up when people told me what my problems were. 'Do you have any problems, Miss Perfect?'

She looked at me with such a direct intensity that I broke eye contact. 'You know what my problem is.'

'Matty?'

She gazed out the net-curtains at the crashing rain. 'Him as well...'

'Why do you go out with him?' I said. I knew it wasn't my business to say stuff like that but felt glad I'd finally asked.

'Good question.' She sighed or maybe it was a resigned laugh. 'I guess I went out with him at the start because he made me feel special; so wanted and safe.'

'Safe?'

'I know it sounds weird.' She bit her lip thoughtfully. 'It's like if there is a chance in life someone barges me out the way and I'm left at the back. It's sort of what you were getting at Regent's Park. People pat me on the head and I smile and do nothing about it. With Matty if anyone disrespected me, he wouldn't put up with it. We were out once and a guy pinched my bum. He made him come up and apologise. It's kind of like he was giving me the respect I didn't have for myself or something like that.'

'What's changed?'

'I've realised I only went out with him for something I didn't have rather than something he did.'

'That doesn't explain why you still go out with him?'

'I go out with him because I'm going out with him.' She laughed and I recognised the type of laugh; it wasn't a release of joy but tension. 'I'm probably a feminist's worst nightmare. Going out with some supposed tough guy because I get pushed around.' The way she said it, with such a flat voice made it seem even sadder.

'I'm no expert but...' I took a long drink of my tea and swallowed, slightly burning my mouth. 'I think feminism is about having the choice about the woman you are, not about being a strong woman.'

She took my hands and clasped them and looked at me but differently. Liz doesn't have an expressive face which is what makes her doll-like and elegant but also very difficult to read. I studied her face for a deeper meaning.

'Do you want anything else my lovelies?' boomed the hearty waitress making us both jump. We released hands instantly like she'd caught us committing a crime.

*

When we finished our teas, we left the cafe and Liz drove me home. We ploughed through the sodden streets, barely a word uttered until we arrived at my house. I said goodbye, got out and stood on the pavement watching until the car disappeared from view.

Each time we met now it was a bit intense and weird – like when we went to Regent's Park. As I walked up the stairs to my flat, I wondered if our relationship had always been that way or whether it was something I'd done. Evidence from all other aspects of my life pointed to the latter.

I unlocked the door and entered the house to find Shell lying in the exact same position I'd left her in. Next to her were a full ashtray and five empty bottles of beer. Up leapt the Dog barking and wagging his tail like he did when he hadn't been walked.

I didn't say anything. Tonight I was going to do two things. Sleep and not argue. I sat down on the armchair across from the couch. 'What did you do today?'

'Chilled.'

'Literally. This place is freezing.'

'I'm lowering our carbon footprint.'

'You mean because if we die of pneumonia we won't be able to fly to Spain again?'

'You do know your jokes aren't funny?'

I did. The lack of laughter was the clue.

The doorbell rang.

'Are you going to get that?' Shell said, sprawling out on the couch and shutting her eyes. Of course I was getting it.

I followed the ringing into the hall and opened the door. Sparky stood before me. 'Oh it's you,' he said, unable to hide his disappointment.

'It is,' I said. 'Sorry for the inconvenience. How can I help you?'

'Errr... I was here earlier and forgot my jacket.'

'You better come in then.'

'Cheers mate,' he said, the odour of old cigarettes following him as he walked past me.

In the living room, he started over-apologising to Shell,

in his whiney-nasal drone, for forgetting a jacket that either didn't exist or that he'd left on purpose. When describing what she'd done all day Shell had conveniently left out with whom she had been doing it with.

'Oh, so you did,' she said, playing along. Still no jacket was visible. 'We'll look for it later... Do you want to stay for a tea?'

'Shell, it's Sunday night,' I said. 'I am sure a cool guy like Sparky has better stuff to do.'

'Don't be daft. Sit down Sparks,' Shell said. 'I'll get you a drink.'

She went into the kitchen leaving us alone in the living room. Sparky lingered next to the sofa, waiting to be offered a seat. I was tempted to make him stand all night but as usual my conscience interjected and ruined my fun. 'Just sit down there where I usually sit Sparky. Yeah, that's right, in my seat. Make yourself at home.'

He sat down and fidgeted as he attempted the impossible: trying to get comfortable on our couch.

Shell returned from the kitchen, 'Guys, there's no milk left. I'll have to pop out and get some. See you in a bit.'

I got up and ran after her. I reached her just before she left the front door. 'What are you doing? Don't leave me alone with him.'

'I'll only be a minute.'

'Wai..,' I said, the closing door drowning out my words. I walked slowly back into the lounge and sat down in the armchair facing Sparky. We looked at each other cautiously – both with no idea what to say. He couldn't put me down because there was no audience: I couldn't ignore him because there was no one else talking. I looked at my watch. Shell had been gone thirty seconds.

'What happened to your eye?' Sparky said, breaking the silence. Even he had better social skills than me.

'I got a knock playing football,' I said. 'You know how it is.'

'No not really. I don't like it. It all seems so trivial.'

I punched the palm of my hand. 'That's too bad...'

'Why?'

'Because if you liked football we could easily fill the time Shell is away talking about it.'

He leaned forward and rested his forearms on his knees and looked at me with a studied intensity. 'Do you not think it says a lot about you that you can only talk to men that like football?'

'Probably,' I said, getting up and turning on the TV. It made the lack of conversation more bearable if no less awkward.

'Are you warm?' I said. 'I keep telling Shell to put off the heating to reduce our carbon footprint.'

'I'm fine. If anything it's a bit cold in here.'

I opened a couple of windows. Perhaps I could freeze him out.

The wind whistled round the room. Dust flapped from the billowing curtains. A motorbike roared down the road. Revellers returned from the pub. Never had time passed more slowly.

Finally there was a knock at the front door. I was on my feet before the last rap, sprinting into the hall. I opened the door and greeted Shell's cheeky smile with a slow shake of my head. Ignoring me, she shouted through to the lounge, 'Hi Sparks. It's milk and sugar isn't it?'

'It's OK I will make them darling. You sit down,' I said, scowling at her.

When I'd made the three cups of tea I opened the fridge and moved the two opened bottles of milk to make room for the third bottle that Shell had just bought. I stopped dead realising what I'd done.

'There was loads of milk and you know it!' I said to Shell, when Sparky had finally left.

'I must have missed it,' Shell said, twisting her dark hair around her finger.

'You left so I would bond with him, didn't you?'

She didn't bother to conceal her amusement. 'Did you?'

'It was one of the worst half hours of my life.'

'I was gone five minutes.'

'Spending time with him is like cat years, you need to times it by eight.'

'He's very talkative and interesting. If it was uncomfortable it was probably your fault,' she said. 'You don't have a very easy manner with people.'

'Thanks, Shell.'

'You'll have another chance to get to know him at the party tomorrow. Who have you invited by the way?'

'Micky and Liz.'

'And Blackie from work,' she added.

'No, you invited him. Anyway, please let's not talk about the party.'

She shuffled up the sofa and studied me. 'What happened to your eye?' She took my right hand. 'Your knuckles are swollen. Have you been fighting?'

'So this party...' I said. 'You're right. We really should talk about it.'

DAY 6

As I settled into my work chair the next morning, I saw that Sarah, the up and coming star of the firm, had walked in right behind me. She sat down at the desk next to me, a smile breaking across her lips. She was a slim, grey-eyed woman, with thick rimmed glasses. Her hair was tied back so tightly it looked like it was strangling her scalp.

Sarah was the type of person who would run up an escalator. She had the gusto of Micky in a club, the keenness of Shell in an argument, the passion of Sparky in front of a mirror. Blessed with the most literal of minds, her main talent was her over-exactness. This made her a brilliant lawyer. Permanently on edge, obedient to the core, she took active listening to a new level, nodding her head constantly, ensuring she was always the first and last to agree.

She'd only been working in the firm for four months but was already displaying all the symptoms of corporate indoctrination. She called the firm 'we'; thought the corporate responsibility programme actually helped people; believed the firm's 'values' actually existed. I liked her a lot but was worried her attitude was having a bad influence on me.

'Hi Zezva. Lovely morning, isn't it?' she said, a hurricane of enthusiasm blowing over my air of disenchantment.

'I suppose so.'

'Did you enjoy Hugh's drinks event the other night?' she said.

I hadn't noticed that she was there. That made me feel bad and so I said, 'Sorry I didn't get the chance to talk to you.'

'We spoke for ten minutes.'

I felt sweat forming on my upper lip. 'I know that... I mean, sorry for not speaking to you longer.'

'That's fine,' she said and smiled with such sincerity that it made me feel even worse. 'Was that your girlfriend who turned up?'

Before I could deny knowing Shell, out of the corner of my eye I saw my boss, Hugh, swaggering in my direction. He didn't say 'hello' or 'how are you?' or 'good morning.' Nothing human like that. He said, 'Zezva, we have a lot of photocopying to do and the secretaries are busy. So can you do it?'

'Yes,' I said, ticking the only available answer box.

*

I stood in the box-like room staring at the mound of photocopying. I tried to convince myself that I was taking the piss, getting paid my wage to do photocopying. But I knew what it meant. It wasn't a real task: it was a message.

You see that's what they do to you in law firms. They don't sack you. They give you the slow handclap. You get less and less work of lower and lower quality. Guess what? You don't reach your target. Guess what not reaching your target is? A sackable offence.

Just when I was wondering if it could get any worse Blackie entered.

He'd been pretty sore about me demeaning his 'deal' in the bar at Hugh's drinks event and had been biding his time for revenge. Here, he had an open goal.

'What you doing?' he said, like he couldn't see.

'Swimming the English Channel.'

He frowned. 'Photocopying like a little bitch more like.'

'Do you want something or are you just here for the conversation?'

Blackie undid the top button of his double breasted jacket and smiled without showing any teeth. 'What's happening with the party tonight?'

'You actually want to go to that?'

'Your girlfriend says it's at the mansion of a local rock star called Sparky and everything is free.'

'Local rock star? She *actually* said that?'

'Yes.'

'Well Blackie, she says a lot of things that aren't true.'

'Why?'

That stumped me so I mumbled some nonsense like, 'Life is a game to her.'

Blackie lowered his prescription free designer glasses and peered at me. 'What type of game?'

'Chess... draughts... polo. Whatever you want. Just don't come to the party. It'll be a big disappointment. Mark my words.'

'I'll take the risk.' He strolled out the room and called over his shoulder. 'See you there.'

I finished the photocopying and returned to my seat, passing Sarah's desk on the way. A note pad sat next to the phone. Every pen had a place; each file was neatly positioned on top of another; not a paper clip was out of place. Sarah leaned on her desk, her head supported by both hands, murmuring gentle sobs. That quickly made me forget about the photocopying and having to put up with Blackie at Sparky's party.

Four years in the Corporate Law game and I'd seen God knows how many lawyers crying at work. Men and women. And still it upset me. 'What's wrong?'

'Nothing,' Sarah said, through sniffs.

'Tell me.'

'I have some urgent work to do on a trademark dispute. I've got five minutes to finish the advice and I'm not close.'

I crouched down to her eye level. 'What makes you think it's urgent?

'Howard said it was.'

'Just because Howard says the word urgent and puts something on your desk doesn't make it urgent. There is no such thing as an urgent trademark dispute. Do your best in the time you have and don't upset yourself.'

'Howard said it was urgent,' she repeated, turning back to face the glow of her monitor. She could hear my words, but couldn't take them in; she could review a 500 page document for a stray word or typo but was incapable of analysing her own existence.

I left her and approached Howard's desk. 'Hi, could I have a quick word, please?'

He continued typing, his thought process too important to break. Thirty seconds later he hit the full stop key and turned. Point proven, big man.

'Yes,' he said.

'I think Sarah is a bit stressed about some work you've given her. She wouldn't say herself but she's a bit stuck. I mean, it must be pretty hard, if she doesn't know the answer.'

Howard looked at me with such intense boredom it was like I'd knocked on his door on a Sunday night to tell him my favourite hobbies included fishing and darts. 'What's your point?'

'The words I just said Howard.' He still looked at me blankly. I was going to have to spell it out to him. 'I think she could do with a bit of help. You are her manager.'

'I explained it very clearly. If she has some questions she knows where I am,' came Howard's automated response. I don't know what I expected him to say. Howard didn't have time to care, and if he did someone would have to pay the firm £500 an hour for the privilege.

*

Shell's moment had arrived.

Yes, I knew she was excited about the party; that she liked to go over the top; that she was impulsive and had a stubborn disregard for her looks. I was also well aware of her constant search for attention and need to feel different. But none of that prepared me for what greeted me when I returned from work.

'Who did that?' I said.

'I did!'

I sat down next to her on the sofa, getting a close-up of her butchered locks. 'Why would you do that to yourself?'

'It's part of my costume?'

'The point of a costume is that you look stupid for one night, not permanently.'

'I knew you wouldn't understand,' she said but was still beaming. My disapproval was exactly what she wanted and she'd got it. 'Admit it. I look exactly like Joan of Arc.'

'Why does looking like Joan of Arc require a hair cut like that?'

'She had short brown hair.' She tutted. 'And you're meant to be educated.'

'I know she had short brown hair. But I didn't know it was at completely different lengths.'

'It was medieval times stupid. She wasn't someone that sat around the house doing her hair all day. She would be out fighting battles.'

And losing them if she was fighting you, I thought.

'Anyway come and look at the costume I've got you.' Shell bounced up from the couch and ran out the door. I followed her to the bedroom where I was greeted by a tousle-haired woman wearing a tunic, pointing with a tin foil musket at a costume laid out on the bed: black tights, a curly white wig, a tube of face paint and the remnants of the white woollen rug my mum had bought us.

'What have you done to my mum's rug?'

'I've cut it up so you can wear it as part of the sheep's costume.'

'How could you?' I said, picking up the shredded material.

'You said you hated it and it was the worst thing in the house.'

'I do hate it. I mean I did hate it.'

'Why do you care if I cut it up then?'

'Because of the memories.'

'You should want to keep things that give you good memories. When your mum bought it for you and you were so ungrateful she started hitting you with it. I remember the tears in your eyes.'

'I have told you hundreds of times. The wool got in my

eyes. I wasn't crying.'

'Anyway you'll get loads of attention and everyone will love it.'

'Will I?' I said. Perhaps it would be nice to be noticed in a good way for once.

'Of course you will. They'll think it's hilarious. Who wouldn't? You can bring the Dog as a prop as well - like a sheep dog.' I looked at the Dog lying in the corner. He didn't look like he wanted to be a prop. 'Anyway Sparky wants to see his dog again.'

'That's thoughtful of him.'

'It is, isn't it?' Shell said without a trace of irony.

*

On arrival, Shell leapt out of the taxi, leaving me to pay the driver. She waited at the front gate and together with the Dog we went up the winding driveway, the house casting us in a deep shade. At the summit a sign attached to a pillar of the porch directed us to the side of the house.

Two men with enormous physiques and psychotic countenances checked the guest list. We gave them our names, passed through the side gate and walked a full seventy paces to the grounds at the back. Shell rushed up the stone steps desperate to catch a glimpse of the scene above. I reached her and stopped next to her. Both our mouths dropped in wonder.

The lawn stretched up, swallowing the distance with its green expanse. There was a swimming pool, a stream, a pond, a table overburdened with glasses of champagne. And people, so many people, dressed in the most stunning of outfits: Cinderella sipping red wine; the Hunchback of Notre Dame tippling whisky from a crystal glass;

Shakespeare pirouetting in his pointy shoes.

Shell had much more important people to see than me so kissed my cheek before hurrying away to kiss half the party on the cheek.

And then I saw a bear lumbering towards me, a cheeky face poking out its head.

'Right for the first time in ma life, I'm delighted I know you. This is a-mazing, man,' Micky said, giving me one of those slappy handshakes he did with the lads at football. I'd never had the privilege of receiving one before.

'Why are you dressed as a bear?' I said. 'You're going to die of the heat in there.'

'Girls love it, that's how. Who are you?'

I reached under the woolly rug that covered my torso and itched my stomach. Whenever I moved I did it slowly in case I ripped the black tights that stretched across my arms and legs. Sweat was already running from under my wig and down my blackened face. 'A sheep... it was Shell's idea.'

'You look like Nelson Mandela.'

'Micky, that's racist and not funny.'

'Don't call me racist. You're the one who's blacked up. It's a wee bit distasteful nowadays.'

We went around in circles both calling each other racist for a couple of minutes before Shell came across to interrupt. 'Hi,' she said, glancing at Micky unable to disguise her scorn. 'Sparks said to tell you that the barbecue will be served soon.'

'Cheers, hen,' Micky said.

'Hen?' Her pierced nose curled. 'Please don't call me that.'

Micky's already densely packed features scrunched up

even more. 'I was being nice...'

'I'll be the judge of that.'

'You wannee know something, Shell? Talking to you is like juggling three hand grenades and a bar of soap.'

She turned to me. 'Zezva, what's he talking about?'

'I've no idea.'

'Sure...' she scowled at me and flounced off.

Micky waited until Shell was out of earshot and drew himself closer. 'She's one scary woman. Listen to me. I've seen it in her eyes. I've seen it before. She's going to flip one day and try to kill someone. It'll probably be you.'

His eyes were big and sincere. He was serious. Well, as serious as someone dressed as a bear could be.

'Thanks, Micky I'll be careful.'

He tapped the centre of his forehead with his finger and nodded. 'Aye, you do that.'

At that point, seemingly from nowhere, Liz had come up and stood next to us. She was wearing knee length socks, a short yellow skirt, and a tight white sleeveless top. Frilly yellow pom-poms were attached to her hands.

'What's this slinky wee thing you've got on?' Micky said.

'I wore this costume to every fancy dress party at university. It's been away for a while but tonight for one night and one night only, the Cornish tart is back,' she said, flicking up the hem of her skirt in mock flirtation.

'You look pure dead gorgeous,' Micky said.

She beamed and looked to me. 'What do you think, Zezva?'

I was going to say exactly what Micky had said - except for the *pure dead* part – but he'd got in first as usual. That threw me because I didn't want it to seem like I was copying him. I did think that the sweat band that swept back her hair made her eyes even more prominent than normal but it would have been weird to say that.

'It's a bit clichéd dressing as a cheerleader, isn't it?' I heard myself say. It was strange that I said that because it wasn't something I felt.

'Thanks a lot,' she said, lowering her pom-poms.

'Don't listen to him. Racists arenae exactly known for their charm. Listen to me, you're a wee stunner.'

She smiled and squeezed Micky's bicep but her eyes flickered towards me. 'I could come to your football matches dressed like this and cheer you on.'

'I wouldnae be able to concentrate. We'd lose every game,' Micky said, so natural around good-looking woman.

'Yes, but,' I strained, desperate to get in on the banter, 'the opposition wouldn't be able to concentrate either so it wouldn't matter.' They both stared at me, unsure of the point I was trying to make. 'It would be a draw,' I concluded, feeling the fabric of the tights prickling my arms.

Micky and Liz exchanged a bemused look and shrugged at exactly the same time.

'OK, Zezva,' she said, in the tone of someone who had lost patience with a child. 'I think I'll have a walk around the party. Do you want me to take the Dog? He's looking a little restless?'

'Yes, please,' I said.

I watched them walk away and felt relieved to be getting rid of two problems at once.

'What was that all about?' Micky said.

'What do you mean?'

'That patter with Liz.'

'I started badly and then didn't recover.'

'It's a conversation not the fucking 100 metres.' He smiled and put his arm around my shoulder. 'Come on ya mad freakazoid, let's get some scran.'

We joined the queue for the barbecue. I could smell the juice of the meat dripping on the charcoal and my mouth watered. Sparky, armed with silver prongs, flipped the food expertly. When we reached the front, he grinned at us and pointed at the naked woman on his apron. What kind of moron would find that funny?

'Class apron,' Micky said and laughed.

'Beer, sun, a naked woman what more do you need?' Sparky said. 'You look like a steak man.'

'Aye, I am. Medium rare.'

Sparky chucked the largest steak on the grill onto a china plate and handed it to Micky with a wink. 'Help yourself to the sundries on the side.' He turned to me with a smirk, 'Sausage, Zez?'

The *sundries* included not only salad but pastas, potato wedges and pizza slices. Just when your plate was full you arrived at the desserts: the fruit salad; the sweet pinks of the blancmange; peach, raspberry, vanilla ice cream.

'Nae wonder you're worried about him,' said Micky, as we settled on the wall of the pond.

'What do you mean?'

'He's like a million times cooler than you.' He cut into his sirloin steak and put a piece into his mouth. 'Brilliant this,' he said, chomping and nodding at the same pace.

I took a bite into my steak, hoping it would taste horrible. Unfortunately it was perfectly cooked, 'It's too good, if anything. It's not what barbecues are all about. They should be more rustic.'

'Admit it. Sparky's a good looking guy, who does a cracking barbecue and throws the best parties ever.'

'No way,' I garbled as I chomped on a deliciously marinated rib. 'I'm eating this out of politeness... oh great.'

'Why are you hiding your face?'

Too late. Blackie had seen us and was sidling over. He was wearing a Top Gun outfit and aviator sunglasses.

'Alright Zezva. Who have you come as?' he said on arrival.

'I'm a sheep.'

'I know that already,' Blackie said, guffawing at his own joke.

Micky laughed along with him and said, 'Love the gear, big man.'

'I'm cheating to be honest. I'm not dressed up. I'm actually a trained pilot.'

'I don't think you've mentioned that before, Blackie,' I said.

'I told you last week - no wonder you're known as the office clown.'

Micky laughed again. With that they started to bond by slagging me off – in the way men do when the only thing they have in common is they both know you.

He's the clown of our football team as well. There's nothing around the office he can't mess up. He's always whinging about things. Yes, nothing makes him happy. He's useless with women. Have you met the one he's with at the moment. Aye, a total nightmare but she's still too good for him.

Fortunately Blackie's innate urge to talk about how expensive his possessions were changed the subject, 'You know this suit costs ten grand?' he said, his mouth was down-turned, eyebrows raised. 'It's a real RAF suit.'

Micky widened his eyes and pointed at Blackie with a quivering finger. 'Hang on a tick. Are you that guy that I saw pulling up in that mint Cayenne earlier?'

'Guilty,' said Blackie, holding his hands up in mock surrender. This show off had really met his audience.

'I've always wanted a ride in one of them. All of ma life.'

'Let's go for a spin then.'

'Are you serious?'

'Sure, let's go.'

With that they left; Micky skipping along at his side, clapping his paws in excitement. They didn't say a word to me. I didn't want to go for a ride anyway.

Alone, perched on the pond wall, I watched the shadows of the trees rippling across the surface. Inside the pond, algae clung to the walls like some form of an aquatic moss. Speckled orange fish zipped across the water, always reaching their destination, going nowhere.

'Zezva,' a thud into my arm. I jumped at the unexpected blow and looked up to see Shell, red faced, fist clenched.

'What darling?'

'Why are you sitting by yourself?'

'I did it so you would hit me in the arm.'

She studied me, 'Why on earth would you –'

'Hey guys. What's up?' Sparky interrupted. I hadn't noticed he'd sat next to me on the wall; he must have slithered over when I was inspecting the other life that inhabited the pond.

'Nothing babes,' Shell said. 'Zezva's being his usual self: thinking he's too good to talk to anyone.'

'Take a draw Zezva. Maybe you'll chill out a bit,' Sparky held out a joint for me to take. I looked at him and thought about how uncomfortable he'd been in the house alone with me and how different he was now that he had his chemical confidence and army of validation.

'I'm fine thanks.'

'Your choice,' he said, like I didn't know it was.

He took another draw and ran his hand through his brown curly hair. If anything these substances seemed to be making him fall more in love with himself. I hoped Blackie didn't get hold of any of it.

Sparky shuffled up the wall and put his arm around me and gave my shoulder a little massage – you know, that way people do when they are about to patronise you. 'You shouldn't think you're better than other people, Zez. That's what you people learn in those places you work in. Tell me, what do you know of Marxism?'

'That it works well at the start but pretty soon the leaders end up living in houses like this.'

'Ah a sceptic - no surprises there.' He smiled. 'Do you even have an ethos?'

'I do actually, Sparks.'

'What is it?'

'That we are only here for a short amount of time and then that's probably it.'

'Yah, absolutely man.'

'So we should try to enjoy ourselves and avoid as many horrible situations and unbearable people as possible.'

'Tot-al-ly, Tot-al-ly,' he said, smoke fluttering from his nostrils.

'Glad you agree,' I said, getting up and walking away. I could hear Sparky spluttering as I left.

I walked around looking for someone I liked: I walked around looking for Liz.

I found her at the bottom of the lawn. She was surrounded by three handsome young men dressed as gladiators, tussling for her attention in the politest of competitions. They all had that look of extreme health: young, white toothed, strong limbed, big footed specimens.

'Oh Zezva, I didn't see you there,' she said. 'Sorry guys, excuse us a second.'

Those charming men, who had been nothing but liked by all those who'd ever met them, watched in wonder as she left them to talk to me.

She led me over to an untaken patch of grass followed by the Dog. 'I've wanted to talk to you all night about the last time I saw you. You know, after football... in the cafe.'

'What happened?'

'When we held each others' hand.'

'What about it?'

'I thought that's why you flipped out earlier.'

'No, I got uncomfortable for no reason. You know the way I do?'

'Yes,' she said quietly.

'Anyway, I should be the one apologising. You looked like you were having a great time talking to those hunks.'

'They were alright. I'd rather talk to you.' To be fair she carried that lie off quite well and even managed to keep her face straight. 'So what have you been doing all night then? Offending people, sulking and thinking about everything far too much?'

That about summed it up but I said, 'No,' for appearances' sake.

'Yes you have been! I know you. Anyway, it's not a bad thing. You're just on a different frequency from everyone else.'

'If I'm ever on the same one as Shell, Sparky or Blackie please tune me out.'

'They're all nice. I can't believe you made out like this would be hell. It's the best party I've been to. That Sparky's a real charmer.'

'Don't you start.'

'You must admit he's pretty cool. He told me he's playing on that stage later. There's a dance floor for people to join in.'

'Well, I'll be waltzing out the door when that happens.'

Sparky, on cue, sprang onto the stage erected at the top of the lawn. He'd taken off his naked woman apron and now wore skinny jeans, white cowboy boots and black spangly shirt fully unbuttoned to reveal his hairy torso. His curly hair flicked out of the bottom of his beanie hat. The thumb of one hand was hooked under his belt; the other grabbed the microphone. His confident voice blasted out of the two amps positioned either side of the stage, 'Hello. Firstly thank you for coming tonight. You've made my, as well as your own, night!' He flapped his hand to the audience as if to say, *please stop laughing... but really don't.*

'But in all seriousness,' he continued, 'I'm going to let you in on something I've been hiding from you all for a while.'

'Your personality?' I heckled.

Those in front turned around and glared at me. Sparky did a great job of pretending he hadn't heard. 'I've been recording an album in secret. This isn't just my annual full moon party. It's the launch of my new record. And everyone is getting a limited edition vinyl for free!'

Bedlam descended. The crowd were out of their minds with happiness. There must have been more drug taking than I'd initially thought.

'Woooo,' Liz said, clapping her pom-poms together. 'That's a nice surprise isn't it?'

'Yes it is a surprise... that anyone could be so vain.'

'How is that vain?'

'It's like giving someone a picture of yourself for their birthday.'

'Guys, calm down,' Sparky said. 'OK...I didn't think it would be appropriate considering the mellow vibe we've created tonight to bring on the electricity. So I'll be treating you all instead to an exclusive acoustic set.'

Twenty minutes later he left the stage to a standing ovation. I saw Shell approaching, her cheeks flushed, the unusual sight of a smile on her face. 'That was amazing,' she said, every vowel over-enunciated.

'It was really gentle and beautiful wasn't it?' Liz said.

'Yes it was. How are you anyway? Are you enjoying the party?'

'Yes, it's brilliant. Oh I love your jewellery by the way. Did you make it yourself?'

'Yes how did you know?'

'It looks so unique.'

'I could make you some if you want.'

'I don't think I would suit it as much as you do.'

Throughout this exchange Liz and Shell were standing very close and pawing at each other in a strange way. I wasn't sure but it looked like bonding. For some reason made me uncomfortable.

'I'm going to pick up my EP,' Shell said. 'I can get him

to sign a copy for you.'

'Oh yes please,' Liz said, rustling her pom-poms together.

Shell hurried off, walking straight to the front of the queue - as was her right being such good friends with the artist himself. She picked up two vinyl records, oblivious to the crushing looks she was getting from the group of arm-folded women next in line.

I watched Sparky signing the covers. One for Shell and one for Liz and could feel the pressure building behind my temple.

'Zezva, what's wrong?' Liz said.

'Nothing.'

'Breathe! You look like you're going to explode.'

'Are you seriously getting the cover signed?'

'Yes.'

'Why do you want him to write his name on a piece of cardboard for you?'

'They are limited editions.'

'Only because no one wants one!'

'I was just being polite.'

'Well don't be! Think. Question things. Don't go along with everyone else all the time!'

I threw my glass on the floor and stormed off.

*

I walked up the garden trying to put as much distance between myself and humanity as possible. At the end of the path, I fought my way through a thicket of brambles to a bench beneath an apple tree. I relaxed my weight onto the rotting wood, a parasol of drooping branches bathing me in shadow.

A panting sound came from the direction I'd come: the Dog. He walked through the apples scattered on the ground, rested against the bench and looked up at me mournfully.

'I didn't ask you to follow me.'

Ignoring me, he averted his eyes to an apple and pawed at it.

The seat, hidden at the very summit of the garden, offered a complete view of the celebrations. The lawn stretched down to the swimming pool; a turquoise stamp in the distance. The barbecue puffed out the last of the charcoal. The turn tables started to spin, releasing great blasts of music through the amplifiers. The dance floor was now full; the most confident mixing with the most drunk.

The sun dipped and the sparkle of the stream became a gurgle in the navy expanse. The full moon rose, kissing the lawn and releasing the inhibitions of the silver revellers.

Then the floodlights came on and the whole scene was lit before me. In the centre of the pool Micky splashed and yelled with delight. My eyes followed Shell this way and that: up the lawn, by the pool, at the bar, flitting from group to group. She seemed untroubled, like everything I characterised her to be was only true when she was burdened with my company.

The whole time I looked for Liz. I was going to go down and say sorry. I was going to tell her she was the last person I was annoyed with. Who knows what else I would have said to her.

But she was nowhere in sight. I thought she'd left. I wish she had. Then a group dispersed at the side of the dance floor, leaving two figures standing alone. Liz was one of them. The other was Blackie. They were dancing too close for people who had just met.

Clasping hands they span, round and round in a dizzying circle. Releasing their hold, they staggered into each other and they drew closer. Grinding to the beat, she clung to his arms, her head resting on his shoulder.

Their movement slowed and they kissed. Not a long kiss; just a missed breath; a sharp fork of pain in the centre of my chest.

A hundred moving bodies and Liz was lost amongst the crowd.

DAY 7

The duvet was pulled away from my body. Light and cold hit me at the same time.

I squinted through half open eyes. My vision filled with one object, Joan of Arc, the smell of alcohol radiating from her mouth. 'GGGEEETTT UUUPPP.'

Mmmm, I replied.

'It's time to change the world!' she said and bounced up from the bed.

I sat up and rubbed my eyes. Shell was now lying on the floor colouring in a piece of cardboard. My tiredness turned to dread: it was the day of the protest.

'What are you doing?' I said.

'Making you a sign.'

'I don't want a sign.'

'This could be the day when you finally realise this is what you want to do with your life.'

'When did you get back from Sparky's party?'

'About ten minutes ago. Right, I'm going to get changed out this gear then we'll leave.'

'But I need a shower,' I said, protesting for the only time that day.

'No time. Hurry up and get ready.' She laid down the marker pen and stood up. 'By the way, what happened to you at the party last night?'

'I came home early in a taxi.'

'Why?'

I got out of bed and shuffled over to the wardrobe and tried to think of something to say – "I stormed out after I saw Liz kissing Blackie," didn't seem appropriate.

'Because the Dog was tired,' I said. It was a lame excuse but Shell didn't seem bothered, which was probably because she was glad that I'd left. Relieved that she appeared to have no further questions, I flicked through the contents of the wardrobe and selected grey clothes that I thought would help me blend into the London background and avoid being spotted. It was putting this ingenious plan into action that reminded me to call work.

'Hi it's Zezva. I'm very ill so I won't be able to make it in today,' I told my secretary, Jayne, putting on the obligatory croaky voice. 'It's flu-like symptoms... A really bad cold and sore bones.... Yes, you heard. Sore bones... Who knows how long. It could be days, weeks or months.' I became conscious that I was getting carried away. 'Or perhaps I'll be fine really soon... OK. See you tomorrow.'

I hung up and turned round to see that Shell had changed out of her Joan of Arc get up. Her jumper was zipped up to the neck; a skull bandana muffled her mouth and nose; her camouflage combats hung off her arse. She brandished a sign in front of my face.

I read the caption,

THE LAW IS IMMORAL

'That's yours,' she said.

'Very catchy,' I said, pausing to let the sarcasm take full effect. 'There is no chance that I'm carrying that by the way.'

'OK, you can have this one then,' she said, handing me another sign.

McFUCKERS

I didn't know if this sign was against Scottish people or fast food. I liked both so picked up, "The Law is Immoral," sign.

*

I sat surrounded by the same capitalist infidels that we were protesting against. A couple of them lowered their FTs to glance at me. My only shield was the 'The Law is Immoral' sign, which ironically was why they were looking at me in the first place.

We alighted at Westminster, exited the tube station and walked towards the march. The short distance to the meeting point gave Shell ample time in which to run through some guidelines. 'One, you need to shout loud and join in the chanting. Two, no violence. It solves nothing. Three, no piss taking. These people take this very seriously. Four, no attacking the police. Unless they start it of course. Five, no spitting, sexism or racism...' She went on listing things I hadn't done in my life until she concluded, 'Finally and most importantly, no lingering at the side, you need to be in the nucleus of the march.'

'Of course,' I said, hoping not to permeate the outer membrane.

*

A bearded, bespectacled man paced across a wooden platform, head bowed like he was unable to bring himself to face the audience.

'Who's that?' I said.

'You know who he is: Ricky,' Shell said. 'As in Ricky's

bar.'

'Ah,' I said, nodding. He was the owner of that awful place Shell and all her mates hung around. I must have seen him slinking around one of the many times I'd been forced to go there. 'What's he doing up there?'

'He's running the protest.'

'Running this protest?' I said, surveying the hundreds of people that surrounded me. 'Shell, he can't even run a decent bar.'

As the words left my mouth, Ricky lifted his head and met the mosaic of colour before his eyes. The crowd raised their placards, the expectant screech of their whistles and horns filling the air. He stood paralysed with fear, a light wind rustling through his shoulder-length hair.

Behind him rose the gothic towers of Parliament, the words of great orators, Churchill, Gladstone and Lloyd George echoing through the majestic halls. To his right, the morning sun was cast upon Westminster Abbey. Beyond this shimmering periphery, unmoved by this crowd or any other, Chaucer and Tennyson, Dickens and Austin, Darwin and Newton, lay in their marble tombs. Now wasn't the time for sound bites but Ricky must have felt the hand of history on his sloping shoulders.

He stuttered a bit at the start but got into the flow as the speech went on. I watched him and despite his shit bar and his dodgy choice of company I wanted him to succeed. This obviously didn't come easily to him but at least he had the balls to do it.

You know, when I think about it now, I realise that the one person in the crowd who should have been listening to him was me. Every word about power structures and inequality and elitism and class and racism described the problems I'd faced the moment since I arrived from Georgia. But my entire life had been an exercise in trying to fit into those structures, not to rebel against them. When I first became a solicitor I thought I finally had...

Perhaps I knew Ricky was right even back then. That all those protesters were right. But I couldn't believe that, let alone show it. I was scared and my fear conquered my principles and I suppose that is one of the many reasons why I'm writing this now.

When he was finished the crowd roared and we trooped away from Westminster towards the Thames. We crossed Westminster Bridge where Wordsworth had stood two hundred years before on the cusp of the very revolution that we were protesting against. Industrialisation had changed London and then the world. The ships of old had gone, yet beneath the bridge the river still glided at its own sweet will. My heart beat faster as the poetry of my own life began to nostalgically rhyme. I moved closer to Shell and put my arm round her. 'Remember we walked down here the first night we met.' I whispered, my lips touching the tips of her ears.

'Not now Zezva,' Shell said, her mighty heart lying still.

'Why?'

'Start chanting,' she said, gesturing manically at me. She hopped away shouting, 'STOP THE GREED' or something like that. She joined a gang of people shouting and wielding placards. This must have been the "nucleus" of the march.

I soon learned the best thing that could happen on the protest was for someone in a passing car to beep their horn or a passerby to cheer in support. This was like hitting a six in cricket or scoring a goal in football. Its effect made the crowd delirious and led to an increase in noise for about ten seconds before the clamour drifted back into the repetitive chanting and kazoo blowing.

I remained at the periphery of the action, my hooded top shielding my face. Viewing the protesters I was surprised to see the majority looked like me; boring people with mundane lives, who had simply had enough of the way things were. Casually dressed, they quietly sauntered through their disapproval. In amongst them were those who marked their dedication to the cause with a bit more panache. One man displayed the talent of riding a unicycle whilst wearing a mask of the Prime Minister. Another, dressed in an over-sized suit, waved a massive cheque for the sum of $10,000,000 made out to the, 'Government's War Fund.'

We crossed the Thames and marched on until we entered Trafalgar Square. A group of Japanese tourists began to take photos. They seemed to view the protest as some form of quaint English street theatre rather than the paradigm changing movement it sought to be. The march left them and their gigantic cameras behind and headed down the Strand towards central London. I was still deciding whether to follow when I noticed Shell barging her way towards me.

'How are you?' she said, brushing aside the sweaty black hair that clung to her forehead.

'I'm fine.'

'You're loving it,' she yelled. I'd never seen her so rapturous.

She linked my arm and we walked together along the Strand until it became Fleet Street; the press houses of old replaced by investment banks, accountancy practices and law firms. The road dipped and forked into two, split by the Bank of England. Missiles deflected off the marble horse that protected the pillared fortress. In the distance the Gherkin pointed upwards like a giant bullet.

We bore left, the sky shrinking as the buildings grew taller. The street narrowed but the crowd grew. Suited men and women watched on, curious but confused, interested but inconvenienced.

'Shell, this march is going towards my office. It better not go past it.'

'I didn't know it was going to go this route,' she said, rearranging the numerous rings that adorned her long thin fingers. If someone as reckless as Shell was visibly worried, there must be a problem.

'I'm getting out of here,' I said, swivelling to see groups of fluorescent jacketed policemen fanning out and ringing the march. The protestors pressed together and all personal space was lost.

'You won't get out now,' Shell said. 'They're penning us in.'

'Why?'

'Here is where it normally gets rowdy.'

*

As I traced my daily movements, I wrestled my way to the centre, hoping that the hub of activity would shield me from prying eyes. The pace dropped. The crowd drove forward, the force of the mass taking me with them towards the police line.

We stopped a few feet in front of them. A stand-off ensued: each side waiting for the other's next move. Young people, mobilised, proud and aggressive, faced each other; similar people with different experiences, cast into two uniformed clans.

A protester stepped too close and was forced back by police baton. The sense of injustice overcame the last semblance of peace. Individualism lost, we adopted the identity of the tribe. If you hit him, I hit you. Punches reigned, batons flailed, riot shields buffed. We weren't fighting someone's husband or brother. We're battling them. The other.

The crowd rushed towards a coffee shop that was the symbol of corporate bedevilment. My body was swept into the current of people and cascaded towards the coffee house.

Boom! We hit the façade and rebounded back.

I struggled free, breaking rank and falling into the police line.

Thwack! A black object struck my head.

Everything slowed down. A warm liquid trickled down my face, claret in colour, saline in taste.

Bodies, movement, an impact, propelled through the window pane of the café. Falling onto a bed of shattered glass. On my back, black dots floating across the spot-lit ceiling. Jazz music purring in the background.

I turned my head and saw an over-shone black boot and suit trouser inches from my face. I grabbed a table leg and tried to pull myself to my feet. My muscles didn't react and my body keeled over, spilling a coffee all over a gentleman frozen in his seat. Must apologize but couldn't focus.

'I've a.... I'm sovvveerree,' I slurred, my mouth not responding to the sentiments of my mind. Wiping away the blood, I covered my eye to aid my view. A balding man sat alone, shaking and holding his wallet up in his surrender. A zap of recognition, before a fellow protester charged past me, picked up the man's laptop and threw it on the ground. The keyboard detached and clattered on my 'The Law is Immoral' sign.

Clumping boots. A dark object lunged at me. A hiss. Liquid gushed into my face. An excruciating sting in the rear of my eyeballs. I grabbed my face and fell to the ground, a thousand shots of pain; a twinge for every shard of glass digging into my body.

A shielded robot loomed over me. Two steel rungs of metal wrapped around my wrists. Click.

*

Penned in, lined up, unmoving, unmoved. Bodies scattered left; bodies swung right. Sub-queues were formed; sub-groups were broken. Some were shouting, desperate to get it over with; others pushed back, trying to escape their unenviable fate.

At the front was a solitary white desk: the pinnacle and the precipice; the gate to the abyss. Once identified and searched, that person was escorted to their quarters and another trudged to the front.

It was my turn. A member of staff guided me by the arm to a man sat behind the white desk, his features sharp, his white hair neatly combed. A pencil thin moustache added sternness to his face. 'Name?'

'Zezva Chichinadze.'

'Can you spell that?'

'Yes.'

He glared at me, 'I wasn't making small talk.'

The officer, who was holding my arm like a jealous

boyfriend, interjected. 'It's OK Serge I have his name here,' he said, producing my wallet.

'Thank you, Constable Clunes,' the Sergeant said, muttering each word through a microscopic slit in his mouth.

'FASCISTS!!!' someone shouted at the back.

I turned to see tens of other protesters, wrestling with police officers in the background. The man who had shouted the invective was being pinned by two burly officers against a wall.

'Look at me,' the Sergeant commanded. 'Right, empty your pockets and place the contents on the desk.'

'With handcuffs on?'

'Remove the handcuffs Constable Clunes.'

Clunes followed his training to the letter by taking my handcuffs off as roughly as he could. I emptied my pockets and dropped the contents on the desk; they had nothing in them except for a couple of notes and a few coins.

'I also have this as evidence,' Clunes announced, producing the 'Law is Immoral' sign as jubilantly as if he'd found the gun that shot JFK.

'Search him,' the Sergeant said.

Clunes gleefully began to pat me down. By the end of the search we were more intimate than I'd been with a number of girls I'd gone out with.

'Very thorough Constable Clunes,' the Sergeant said, raising one of his eyebrows with agonising exertion. He turned his head and looked at me like I was the closing scene of the most boring film he'd ever seen. 'Constable Clunes tells me you've received a defensive blow to the head and also been pepper sprayed whilst attacking a man in a coffee shop. Now I'm obliged to ask you if you have any symptoms from this.'

'What answer gets me out of here the quickest?' I said.

'Saying, "No, I'm not suffering from any symptoms especially dizziness or double vision."'

'I'm not suffering from any symptoms especially dizziness or double vision,' I said, addressing the middle of the faces crossing over in front of me.

'Good. Now I must inform you that you've been arrested on suspicion of criminal damage and assault,' the Sergeant said. 'Please follow Constable Clunes to the cells.'

Clunes led me through an arch of chrome. Click. Slam. Into a corridor. Up some stairs to a further corridor, the passage getting brighter the deeper we went into its webbed labyrinth. Click. Slam. The luminous tubules above beat sweat out of my brow, their unremitting buzz like a swarm of hornets stinging my brain. Reaching our destination, Clunes pushed me into a room and sealed the metallic door, turning my world from neon to black. Click. Slam.

On my hands and knees in the centre of the cell, I sucked in the stagnant air; each breath was as repulsive as the last. The walls of the cage compressed, pushing down, up, and in. Guided by touch I found a bench, and manoeuvred onto its cold, hard support.

My head was too tender to lay down, too heavy not to collapse. Giving in, I lay on the bench; stuck in a head of ringing ears, burning irises, throbbing cerebrums; a rocking cradle of turbulence; a timeless montage of spinning ceilings and walls.

DAY 8

I laid there on the bench in the police cell and slept but dreamt that I was awake. When I awoke I thought I hadn't been asleep. After what felt like hours, I dropped off.

A sharp clicking sound and the grind of the opening door brought me back. Then the light changed and everything was white, except for a shadow, moving towards me. The words reached me one by one, 'It's time to go.' A uniformed man glowered at me. 'Get up and follow me.'

I hauled myself off the bench, staggered out of the door and trailed him back through the maze of corridors. As I did, my mind reacquainted itself with reality as blobs of mass morphed into walls and doors, desks and chairs.

By the time we'd reached the Custody desk, my vision had almost cleared. The thin-lipped bureaucrat of before had been replaced by a chubbier man, with black rimmed spectacles resting upon his cheeks.

'Right, Mr Chichinadze we are releasing you without charge,' he said. 'You're lucky that you're not worth the paperwork.'

'Charges, no?' I managed, my brain not yet connected to my mouth.

'Charges? Me charges no. Are you a caveman Chichinadze?' Laughter rumbled from the depths of his enormous frame.

I squinted at him and wondered if he was laughing at what he had just said or whether I'd missed something and my hearing was also damaged.

Seeing that he was getting nothing from the quivering wreck propped up by his desk, the custodian gave up and decided to play it straight. 'The coffee company do not wish to pursue the matter due to the negative publicity and we've received no complaint from the man you assaulted, so you are free to leave. Please sign this form and we'll return your property.'

The fact I hadn't assaulted anyone and that the police themselves had pushed me through the window seemed to be neither here nor there. The custodian produced two see-through evidence bags from under the desk, unsealed them and earnestly laid twenty something pounds and 'The Law is Immoral' sign on the counter.

'OK, you are free to leave. Follow Constable Johns and he'll show you out. I hope you enjoyed your stay, please don't return soon.'

As I stepped out the station my head felt like someone was kicking my brain. I looked down at my t-shirt, ripped and speckled with blood and then up at the sky. The light was bright like it was early to mid afternoon.

I don't know what made me do the next thing. Maybe it was the concussion or the lack of sleep and food. But for whatever reason I decided to head straight to work. I reasoned that the sooner I went there the less likely it would be that they'd notice my absence or question my sickie the day before.

*

I pushed myself through the revolving glass doors of the entrance to my office. All I needed to do was get to my desk, pick up my spare suit, get changed and continue as if nothing had happened.

The eyes of both security guards followed my movement across the foyer. I nodded in that way you do to unfamiliar men who look tough: trying to combine friendliness with a touch of machismo. They didn't return my acknowledgement. Instead they looked at me, looked puzzled, looked at each other and then back again at me. Ignoring them, I strode on to the lift and pressed the button. I squinted through my good eye at the row of clocks hosted above the lift shaft. It was 9pm in Beijing, 9am in New York and 5am in Los Angeles. Most worryingly it was 3pm in London.

That confused me. Had I been in the station for over 24 hours or for 2 hours? The lift arrived and the doors opened to reveal two suited people. As I stepped inside, they declined my eye contact and instead exchanged peculiar glances. After some polite coughing the woman removed a handkerchief to cover her nose. The man covered his mouth with his hand.

Bing. The 7th floor.

I left the lift and walked to my desk, focusing on the golden line that ran along the maroon carpet. I sensed an approaching force and looked up to see a mass of orange files bobbing towards me. Dodging to the right, I clipped the top file with my shoulder, causing the rest to crash onto the floor. One thump, two thumps, then three, followed by a scream nine octaves above middle C. And there was Jayne, my secretary, with files strewn round her high-heeled feet.

A scrawny woman of forty, Jayne was so thin she looked like she was walking through an x-ray machine. She combined this gauntness with being perpetually pregnant - giving her the appearance of an anaconda that had swallowed a zebra. Her pedantic lips were always moving. I had more than a vague suspicion that Jayne didn't like me. I had no suspicion as to the reason why.

The commotion of the file spillage had already attracted the full attention of the bored workers.

'It's your files I'm carrying over here. It's a disgrace you're making a pregnant woman carry so many things in the first place without barging into me,' Jayne said. Her fellow secretaries murmured their support from their desks.

'Attacking pregnant women again, Zezva?' Blackie roared from his vantage point.

'It was an accident,' I said, scrambling round the floor, trying to quell the uprising whilst placing the loose papers back in their folders. 'And I didn't ask her to carry these things.'

'What's that smell?' Jayne said, her craggy nose pointing towards the ceiling.

'How am I meant to know?' I said, becoming more flustered - even Sarah was peering round her desk to see what was going on.

'Why are you wearing a t-shirt that's too small with the tags still on?' Jayne said, peering at the cheap t-shirt I'd bought on the way to work.

'So I can take it back to the shop when I've put my suit on.'

Her lip curled in disgust. 'Have you got blood your face?'

'Do you actually think I would come to work with blood on my face?'

She looked at me, standing there with blood on my face and must have decided it was so unlikely that I actually had blood on my face that, in fact, her eyes must be deceiving her. She even mumbled, 'Of course not.'

After I'd helped her pick up the files, I headed for the sanctity of my desk, passing Howard on the way. As usual he was transfixed by his monitor - his indifference for once working in my favour. I unhooked the spare suit and shirt from my filing cabinet and headed towards the male changing area.

But by then the news of my arrival had reached the regal section of the office. Hugh had clambered off his throne and was advancing in my direction. He froze for a moment when he set his beady eyes on me, legs spread, his hands twitching by his side. We faced each other, twelve feet apart. Breaking the deadlock, he walked past me, his five foot four frame thwarting his attempted stride. He called over his shoulder, 'Zezva, a word.'

I followed him into the glass-panelled meeting room. He was already seated, veins bulging from his scrawny neck. 'Do you think it's acceptable to come to the office with blood on your face, smelling like you haven't washed in days? What if a client had seen you?'

'The world would probably have imploded and we'd all have died.'

'Your unprofessionalism is unbecoming.'

'As unbecoming as all of them looking in?' I said, drawing his attention to the plague of colleagues gathering outside, eager to see a fellow 'team' member fail. Although my animated gestures had no effect, a dismissive flick of Hugh's hand sent them all scuttling back to their computers.

'Give me one reason why I shouldn't sack you?' Hugh said, moving his chair closer to mine. I instinctively moved further away, maintaining the four feet, and entire perspective on life, that separated us.

'This is not a career Zezva it's a lifestyle,' he went on. 'You can't come into this office and then go against all the values of the business as soon as you leave it. Please explain why you pretended to be ill and went to a protest?'

'To please my girlfriend and stop us breaking up.'

'Zezva, do you think chucking yourself through windows is the answer?'

'I didn't chuck myself through the window to impress my girlfriend. Although it probably would have done if I did,' I said, adding my compulsory needless aside. And then I paused. One by one the topics of Hugh's questions (the protest, being arrested, the smashed window) registered. 'How do you know all this, anyway?'

'I was sitting having a coffee going through the Project Beta file when you and your mob came crashing through the window.'

'That was you?'

'You know fine well it was me. I can't believe you did nothing when your cohorts attacked me.'

That was a strange comment: when had I ever given Hugh the impression that I would have intervened to stop someone attacking him?

'Irrespective of lying about being ill,' he continued, 'those protests are immoral and we don't condone them.'

'As immoral as going to a strip bar on the company credit card like Blackie does?'

'How can you compare your actions to that? Jonathan takes our clients out and shows them a good time. It's legal and good for business. Your actions were illegal and bad for business,' Hugh said, reacting like I had compared the Virgin birth to gangster rap.

'Hugh, you can't judge an act of morality on how much money it makes you.' I said, speaking with the candour of a man who was certain to lose his job.

'How dare you question my morality. If I'm not here providing a legal service, I'm at church helping others.' He straightened his tie and puffed out his chest in the manner you'd expect of a man of such morality. 'The first step on your road to redemption is to come to a meeting with Smith and Simmons. I know you've been dealing with them and for some unknown reason they like you and want you in their meetings. Go and have a shower, put your suit on and I'll see you on the 5th floor in an hour,' he said, not letting my 'immoral' behaviour get in the way of a couple of chargeable hours. 'If anyone asks about your face say it was rugby or corporate boxing.'

'What's corporate boxing?'

He sighed. 'Just say rugby, Zezva,'

*

I stared into the mirror for the first time in days. A technicolour bruise of yellows, greens and purples had formed on my swollen eye from football; a black bag of fatigue hung from the other. Wrinkles scratched across my forehead. My dark, curly hair was even more wild than usual. Black dots sprinkled my jaw-line and upper lip, creating a shadow across my sallow complexion. I was sure I used to get complimented on my smooth, olive skin.

I washed the blood from my face and put on my spare suit that I hadn't worn in months. It was massive on me, which was strange because I'd had it tailored only six months before. I waded out the changing room, drowning in linen.

Blackie met me at the door of the meeting room. It looked like he was going to be in this meeting as well. Great.

'Zezva,' he said with a smile.

'Blackie,' I said with a scowl.

'Not seen you in a while. Love your dad's suit.'

'Thanks. I love your mum's breakfasts.'

'Touché,' he said, giving me a lopsided smile. 'Not seen you in a while. Did you enjoy Sparky's party?'

'No, I hated every moment.'

'I know... I know... it was marvellous, wasn't it? By the way, what's the name of that fit blonde you knock around with? One minute, she was all over me. The next she just snaps, starts crying and goes home. Wouldn't give me her number or anything. You hang around with some right weirdos.'

I looked at him and considered if I should punch him and knock his whitened teeth down his throat or if I should grab his blood red tie and strangle him. I was stepping towards him when Hugh appeared. 'Hello boys, come in and meet the clients,' he said, full of pride like we were orphans he'd adopted and nurtured to adulthood.

As we entered the meeting room two men rose and moved around the table to greet us. One was a man, who walked like he was leaning back, his stomach pushed out like a giant buffer. The other was a tall man with a bald head.

'Rob and Mark you know Zezva,' Hugh said. 'Also please meet the upcoming star of the firm, Jonathan Black,' said Hugh, standing next to Blackie oscillating between figurative and literal back-slapping.

'Blackie! I remember you. You're a bit of a ladies' man, aren't you?' said Rob, making Blackie's year. Blackie is the type of ladies man that everyone knows - a self professed one.

'I say Zezva are you OK?' Mark said. 'You look a bit worse for wear.'

'Well you wouldn't be at your finest if you'd spent the night in jail.'

Mark yanked at his earlobe and leaned towards me, 'In jail, you say?'

'Yes, don't worry,' I said. 'I was just doing some corporate boxing in there.'

Hugh laughed and put his hand on my shoulder, his feigned affection full of menace. 'Why don't you go and get some coffees from the canteen Zezva,' he said, perhaps considering the sacrilege that my attendance wasn't worth the money he was earning from it.

'It's OK I'll go,' Blackie said, blind as usual to any nuance.

'No, Zezva will go,' Hugh said, pointing to the door in case I didn't know where it was.

I left the room and didn't go back, of course. Get the coffees was code for kindly fuck off and that's what I did.

I walked back to my desk and sat down.

You see, the thing about Hugh is that he didn't really care what I did outside the office (despite all his earlier posturing) as long as I could still perform at work. The meeting was a test. I'd failed.

When the meeting had finished Hugh walked past my desk, 'Zezva, don't come in for the rest of the week. Sort yourself out. Change your attitude or change your job.'

In the lift on the way out, I squinted at the floors ticking down and massaged the bump that had formed on my head. Through the fatigue and headache and hunger and thirst my rage became confused. I was still angry with my football team for not sticking up for me; with the police for arresting me; with those mindless functionaries in the office; but most of all I was angry with Shell who was angry with my football team, my job, the police and my work. Trying to decide if there was anyone in my life who I didn't detest or who didn't dislike each other made me even more furious with Shell, who I blamed for all the hatred.

I left the building and walked to the tube station, heading to exactly where I knew she would be.

*

An open handed fist.
Ricky's bar door rebounds off its hinges.
The room is full but I can only see one person.
Sitting on a beanbag in the corner.
I stride to her.
'Shell, I need to talk you.'
'Go on then.'
'In private.'

'In this community we have no secrets.'

I stare at her. She knows these eyes and when to listen and she does. Up she stands, flouting her displeasure as she follows me to the exit.

The one-time lovers face each other in the street.

'Where the hell have you been? I can't believe you left the protest without saying anything.'

'Do you know I got arrested and spent a night in jail? I almost got sacked today because of you.'

'You jailed for the cause? Really? I'm so proud of you!'

She smiles at me for the first time in weeks. I can see the decay on her teeth.

'Zezva! Wait until I tell everyone in there. That'll change their opinion of you.'

I grab her shoulders. My arms straighten and I hold her still. 'WHY WON'T YOU UNDERSTAND? I DON'T CARE WHAT THEY THINK ABOUT ME.'

'You have two seconds to let go of me, Zezva.' *She kicks at my shins.* 'And if you don't care what my friends think that means you don't care what I think.'

'YOU'RE RIGHT - I DON'T CARE WHAT YOU THINK.'

I let go of her.

She walks backwards wagging her finger at me. She nods her head and turns back into Ricky's.

*

Back in the house, I peeked through the curtains. No one in sight. Nothing happening. No Shell.

I paced over to the mantle piece and picked up Aunt Tiesa's fake gold clock. Roman numerals and bad news. Over two hours since the argument outside Ricky's. The anger had faded; all that remained was a throbbing in my head and the feeling of regret.

This was how it felt to alienate everyone in your life.

A lap of the room. Pacing my problems away. The Dog asleep on the couch. Glancing at my phone. A moth tortured itself against a light bulb; millions of years of evolution defeated by electricity. Sitting down and scrolling through the TV channels. People eating maggots in a jungle. Flick. A stern faced cop over-acting. Flick. A politician complaining about immigration. He had my vote. I wished they'd banned us all a long time ago. Twenty years ago to be precise. Another look at the phone and I gave in. I rang Shell.

'Hi, it's me. You're late. Where are you?'

'I'm not coming home tonight. I feel intimidated by your aggressive behaviour outside Ricky's. I've talked to everyone and we think it's best I keep away from you whilst you're in such a violent mood,' Shell said, her words and tone showing she was speaking as much for the audience as me.

'You know fine well you've nothing to be scared about.'

'I'll be the judge of that.'

'Where are you going to stay?'

'Sparky's house.'

'Sparky's?! Oh right I get it. Finally found an excuse have you?'

'Yes, I have actually.'

'Well just stay there forever.'

'I will.'

'Come and pick up your stuff tomorrow and don't come back.'

'With pleasure.'
She hung up.

DAY 9

I went to bed thinking about my job and Shell and where it was all going and where it had been. I lay rigid and awake. Why was I trying to sleep? Why didn't I accept it was something that I couldn't do?

So I did what I do when the insomnia is this bad: I got up and roamed. The sleepless do this. I don't know why. Perhaps if we are moving it's like we aren't trapped. Or it could be our way of regaining control - like we've chosen to be awake rather than it being imposed on us.

If I say that I walked all night, the Sleepers won't believe me. But I did. And they won't believe it felt like rest either. But it did.

At night the scene changes with the colours of the sky. When it's at its darkest there are shouts and laughs and screams and arguments, as revellers gather outside bars and clubs. These people are Sleepers but out late and drunk. They won't be there tomorrow. They choose to be there. And when the sky pales they leave towards their hangovers and stories about crawling home at four in the morning.

Then the half hour happens- before one day ends and another one begins: not midnight but the real change. The moment before dawn, when the streets become quieter and the only ones who inhabit them are the terminally discontent. Winos dry out in allies, druggies search for fag ends, old men rustle in bins, insomniacs wandering through their tiredness.

The light pushes upwards and the world ends and starts again. That's when the postmen, the milkmen, the poorest shopkeepers, the street cleaners and the suited workaholics join the fray.

It was dark that moonless night when I left the house. At the end of the road a gang of youths hung around a twenty four hour garage, hoods up, heads down. The forecourt was bright. The owner of a souped up Fiesta adjusted his sunglasses and reattached his fuel cap. The attendant looked on from behind the bullet proof glass. He couldn't feel the cool breeze or hear the light shower that pattered onto the yellow and red roof. The dim street lights reflected off the wet street; puddles of yellow light broken by my boots.

Soon the Sleepers were gone and there was nothing and no one, not even a drop of rain. It was the time I've talked about: when we have the world to ourselves, that short moment before dawn.

Then the shutters of shops clattered upwards. Newspaper boards grated along the street. The morning painted the clouds a soft red. The red disappeared, fading into the blue dome that covered the city.

And all night no one noticed me. I realised that I was everything to me but a speck to everyone else and that that was the problem with my life and everyone else's: we couldn't comprehend how insignificant we were to everyone but ourselves.

The sun was high now and warmed my back. The dew melted into the grass and perfumed the air. The clipping sound of high heels. A girl in a silver top and mini-skirt wearing the previous night's clothes. She hid her face, perhaps ashamed. She couldn't see I didn't care. She was a speck - just like me.

I don't decide to go home. I just go. When I get in, my feet hurt and the house is lifeless and pale and I wonder if I've been sleep-walking and if it all happened or whether I was dreaming and sitting on the couch all along.

I waited until a time when normal people get up and phoned Liz. I didn't want to call her after seeing her kissing Blackie at the party but I couldn't stop myself.

She was on the bus on the way to work. I pretended I was commuting because I didn't want to tell her I was suspended from work.

She asked me if I wanted to play tennis that night, which was a very Liz thing to do. You know, nice and gentle and fun but kind of boring. But I thought why not. I spent the afternoon in the house waiting. Waiting for sleep to hit me or for the caffeine to kick in; waiting for another day to pass me by; waiting for Liz.

*

Shielded by a leafy canopy, I followed the trail and listened to the twang of the strings and the cluck of cleanly hit balls. Pebbles crunched beneath my trainers and the brilliant light expanded with each step. The path dropped, widening into a clearing, revealing eight grass tennis courts.

A reclining lawn provided views of the games unfolding below. On these emerald plains, the haves and have mores of society, lolloped in the evening sun.

Inside the clubhouse, the facilities were more reminiscent of a high class restaurant than a sports complex. The members sat around glass tables, wearing all-white costumes and sun glasses. The women socialised; one hand on a glass of Pimms, the other cocked in the air flicking out various gestures. They didn't converse but instead nodded incessantly whilst yelping 'ya, ya' like a pack of over-evolved seals. Clusters of white males formed separate groups, ignoring each other, foreplaying with their phones.

I saw Liz approaching from across the restaurant. Her hair was tied into two bunches. She wore a tight polo shirt and a pleated skirt. The thought of what a great body she had arrived in my head but I dismissed it. It wasn't my place to be thinking things like that. Especially after what she'd done. But I'd promised myself not to mention that.

When she reached me I made sure we didn't do any of the usual hugging and kissing nonsense and kept it to simple hellos.

'What have you got on?' I said.

She looked down at herself and frowned. 'What do you mean?'

'You look like you're going to a fancy dress party dressed as a tennis player,' I said without thinking. But then I did think about fancy dress parties and Sparky's fancy dress party and seeing Liz kissing Blackie. I tried to hold my promise to keep quiet but couldn't really get it out of my head after that.

'You're one to talk. What's that sweat band on your head?' she said

'It's not a sweat band,' I said. 'It's a bandage.'

'I thought those football players only gave you a black eye.'

'No, it wasn't them that did this. I fell through a window protesting against capitalism with Shell.'

She studied me closely for any hint of ridicule. She started to nod her head and jab me in the ribs with her racket, 'Will you stop taking the piss for once?!'

She clearly didn't believe me. It wasn't exactly a story that made me look good so that was fine by me. I changed the subject. 'Anyway, I thought this game was going to be a knock around in the park not a visit to the high court of society.'

'I told you it was here.'

'You said it was public courts.'

'I told you twice it was a private club that I'm a member of.'

'OK let's leave it,' I said 'No one wins in these conversations about who said what.'

'Unless one person sent that person a message telling them it was a private club and to wear white and the other person replied and actually has worn white.'

I was certain I didn't get a message or reply but I suppose she had a lot on her mind or something so must have forgotten. I took a long drink of my can of energy drink. It was my fourth of the day. These drinks really were over-rated or had no effect on me.

'Why are you drinking that? Have you not been sleeping well again?'

How did she know? She was so sensitive to everything I did or didn't do. I wasn't sure if I liked that or not. Either way I couldn't get anything past her. 'I slept fine thanks,' I said and tried to look vibrant and not tired.

'That's why you're forgetting things, isn't it?'

I sucked air in through my nose and breathed it out slowly. 'Like you keep forgetting to mind your own business?'

The lightly freckled skin on her nose creased. 'I wish you'd stop snapping at me all the time.'

'All the time?'

'You snapped at me and stormed out of Sparky's party.'

I looked at her standing there in her little tennis costume in all her mock innocence and thought why does she need to bring this up? But I remembered my promise and didn't react. 'I had a very stressful night.'

'You were at the party of the year, not being tortured.'

I was going to leave it but I couldn't let that pass without a comment. 'It looked like you were enjoying yourself.'

'I was.'

'Liz, I know.'

'Know what?'

I couldn't hold it in any longer. 'I saw you kissing Blackie.'

Her eyes shot downwards. Two turquoise saucers smashing off the ground. 'I thought you'd left.'

'What does it matter if I did?' I said. 'It still happened.'

Her face was taut as she lifted her head and looked out the windows towards the tennis courts. She began to shake her head. Slow at the start but getting faster like she was trying to undo it all with a movement of her head. 'I thought you'd left,' she repeated, her words barely audible.

'Alright, just forget it. Come on, let's go and play tennis,' I said. I'd made my point and the tension was becoming uncomfortable.

We walked out of the clubhouse, across the viewing hill to the gate of the courts. I thought I'd got away with it but then all of a sudden she grabbed my arm and said, 'Before we go on...'

'I've told you, you don't need to explain to me.'

'I know you don't mean that. I can see it in your eyes.'

'You can't see anything in my eyes. How long do we have the court for?'

'An hour.'

'I've come all this way for an hour?!'

'I told you that in the message.'

She was really taking advantage of these supposed messages she'd sent. I was going to say something but then she adjusted the sweatband that covered her wrist.

'What are those bruises?'

She unlatched the gate to the court. 'Judo...' She swallowed. 'They're from my judo class.'

'Since when did you do judo?'

She looked at me then like she wanted me to say something. When I said nothing, she turned to the court and muttered, 'Since always.'

She probably messaged me that too...

*

I sat on the grass half-watching the other matches. Liz approached holding two pints of squash. She gave me my glass and sat down next to me.

We'd stopped playing twenty minutes before but I was still sweating. I downed the juice and wiped my forearm across my face but still the sweat wouldn't stop.

'Have this,' Liz said, taking out a white towel from her bag.

I took it and wiped it over my face and arms and my hair and then looked at it. It was a weird yellow colour, which was strange because I thought when she gave it to me that the towel had been white. I looked at Liz and she straightened her face but I think I saw a hint of disgust. Before I could question it she said, 'What just happened?'

'What do you mean?'"

'Well, we've played tennis loads of times and I've never beaten you before, let alone 6-1.'

'It was a bad day.'

'You fell over twice. You were doing air shots. You forgot the score every point. You kept walking to the wrong side.'

I rubbed my head with the towel and said, 'There are too many rules in tennis. I can't remember them all.'

'You don't have much problem usually.'

I sat up and glared at her. 'Liz, I've been in prison, punched, maced, pushed through a window, almost lost my job. I've not slept in... I can't even tell you what day is. And that's not even mentioning breaking up with Shell. I come here trying to take my mind off it and all you do is whinge about my tennis skills.'

'I'm not worried about your tennis, you dummy. I'm worried about you.' She softened her voice and said. 'What's all this about protests and arrests?'

'I don't want to talk about it.'

'Has Shell really left you?'

Then came the interrogation: why did you break up? It was a misunderstanding. Over what? Everything. When? Yesterday. Why didn't you tell me? I haven't seen you. Where is she now? At Sparky's house not answering my calls. Is it permanent? Who knows. Do you want it to be? I don't know. Why don't you know? Because I never do. Were you ever completely happy with her anyway?

I wanted to put an end to this grilling so I said, 'Look, I'm probably not going to be completely happy with anyone. It's me not her.'

'Zezva, there are people out there who make others happy; who love to spend every moment of the day with each other; people who would wake up every morning excited to be lying next to you.'

'Lying next to me?'

She bit her lip and her face reddened, 'I mean, in general.'

She was right. I should be sorting out this mess with Shell rather than sitting there talking about it. I stood up.

'What are you doing?'

'You're right. I'm going to go to Sparky's to see her. Thanks for lending me the racket.'

'Are you sure that's a good idea when you're so agitated? Maybe calm down and go home instead.'

'Stop going on about me not being calm. I'm completely relaxed.' I started to walk backwards. 'Right I'd better go. See you later.'

I lifted my hand in goodbye as I backed away and turned and left her sitting on the now sunless hill.

I walked up the wooded path and left the club. I walked a hundred metres down the road and reached the bus stop. About a minute later a red double-decker bus pulled in. I got on and sat downstairs near the front.

Further down the line the type of man who frequented many a London transport system embarked. He wore a sandwich board that said, "Jesus Forgives You." He stood at the front of the bus, arms outstretched, lamenting the sinful lives that we inhabited and embraced. 'Let Christ save you,' he impeached, his hands shaking, electrified by his faith. Deliciously mad, he was desirous of nothing but the one thing no one would give him: the time of day.

After about five minutes, he gave up, slumped onto the seat next to me and breathed out a lungful of angst.

My phone started to vibrate in my pocket. I took it out and saw Liz's name flashing on the cracked screen. I hated speaking on buses so I let it stream to answer phone. A minute later the bus pulled into my stop. 'Good luck,' I said, patting the preacher man on the back, painting a smile all over his face.

'God bless you,' he shouted after me.

I got off and listened to the answer phone message Liz had left.

'Hi, sorry about earlier. You know I'm worried about you. But I don't think there is any need to be so mean to me. You made me cry. I've been having a bad time of it lately. I don't want to talk about it on the phone. I didn't really take up Judo.' Her breath billowing down the speaker. 'Also I know you're annoyed about the Blackie thing but I don't regret doing it. Not after what Matty has done. The only thing I regret is that you saw. That's all. OK. Bye. Oh and let me know how it goes with Shell. Bye.'

I felt bad listening to that message even though I didn't know what it meant. It was the tone of her voice as much as what she'd said. I continued down the street and flicked through my phone and saw all the messages that she'd said she'd sent earlier. They were marked as read but I couldn't remember seeing them. I left the main road and vowed to phone her back after I'd found and spoken to Shell.

As I walked to Sparky's house chestnut trees threw deep shadows across the boulevard. Ivy bushes crept through the gaps in the iron fences. I sucked in the clean air of the London countryside and walked until I reached

Sparky's place, perhaps the largest house on the street. I walked up the steep driveway to an enormous oak door framed by two limestone pillars and a stained-glass window. I stepped into the porch and pressed the door bell, releasing a powerful eruption within - a foreboding double bong probably originally designed to attract the attention of the most indolent servants. From inside, I could hear footsteps approaching and Sparky's muffled voice shouting, 'Is that the pizzas?'

'No, it's me, Zezva.'

The door opened. Sparky was wearing a pair of Superman Y-fronts and a white vest. His body sprouted the same curly brown hairs as his head. Sweat dripped off his sunbed tanned skin.

'Is Shell in?'

'No, she's gone back to your place,' he said.

'That's so annoying. I've come all the way here.'

'Well, you should have called her...' Sparky put one hand on the doorframe and leant against it, probably imagining himself as conveying some sort of lackadaisical swarthiness. He looked into the house and then back at me as if to say, *is that all?*

Realising I was getting nothing but a lesson in smugness, I said, 'Can you tell her I called?'

'Sure.'

I turned to leave. Two steps and it hit me.

I spun back around. 'Pizzas? Pizza*sssss*.'

'What are you talking about?'

'Plural, Sparky. Fucking plural.'

He screwed up his face. 'Plural what?'

'When I got here you shouted, "Is that the pizzas?" The pizza*sssss*.' He looked fairly cool until I started walking towards him hissing *pizzas* like some kind of Italian Hannibal Lector.

'What are you doing?' he said, frantically trying to shut the door.

I shouldered the door open and its weight threw Sparky backwards. He fell into a table and then onto the floor. The table crashed down next to him as did a white vase, which had been displayed on the table.

I stepped over him and pieces of shattered china and ran upstairs towards the sound of the love making music, which that rat had been playing whilst he was seducing my girlfriend. Into the bedroom, I saw a human form hiding beneath the covers. I strode to the bed and ripped off the sheets and wasn't surprised when I revealed a naked woman. That the woman wasn't Shell was more of a shock.

She grabbed the duvet and pulled it back over her and released a high-pitched scream.

'Please calm down. I thought you were someone else.'

'Get away from me,' she yelled, the veins in her neck bulging.

Hearing a groaning behind me, I turned to see Sparky shuffling into the room, clutching his right hand with his left.

'Sparky, please tell her to stop screaming and that I thought she was Shell.'

'Are you joking you maniac?' he stalked towards me, appearing taller and broader than before.

I backed away, uncertain of his next move. 'Look, let's remember you're a pacifist.'

'Well you're not. Look at my fingers. They're definitely broken,' he said, lifting his hand. His index and ring fingers were splayed outwards.

'Dislocated,' I corrected.

'That's worse!' he said, his voice shrill and echoing around the high ceiled room. 'And stop pulling that face.'

'What face?'

'You look disgusted.'

'Sorry, it's just I'm a bit squeamish and your hand is pretty gross,' I said. My last comment really riled him. The woman in the bed had gone very quiet as well, which further unnerved me. I began to thumb towards the door, 'I really should...'

'YES,' Sparky and the woman said in unison.

I walked backwards giving Sparky a wide berth as I did. I stopped at the door. 'Before I go we should talk.'

They both looked at me like I was an affront to mankind.

'OK... I'll do the talking. I think that we all agree what I've done is pretty out of order. So we need to think about how to fix this. I'm really sorry for exposing you and frightening you when I burst in,' I said in all sincerity to the woman in the bed. 'I promise not to remember anything I saw.'

'How are you going to do that?' she said.

With great difficulty was not the right reply so I moved it on. 'Sparky, I'm sorry for hurting your hand,' I said, again with sincerity but perhaps a little less. 'OK, in terms of reparations,' I relaxed a little: I was a lawyer after all so this was more my area of expertise than trauma counselling. 'From my side I'll pay for any damage –'

'That vase is probably worth £15,000,' Sparky said.

'If you'd let me finish,' I tried to keep an even expression. 'Any damage not covered by home insurance.'

Sparky looked like he wanted to speak but was clearly so furious he couldn't. I took advantage.

'Right, agreed!' I said, clapping my hands together like it sealed the deal or something. 'OK, from your side perhaps it would be better to never tell Shell about this... you know... ever.'

A deep scarlet seeped across his skin. 'LEAVE NOW.'

Well aware that anger and pain were a deadly combination, I backed out of the door.

*

I reach my street as the sun dips beneath the horizon, bursting crimson across the sky. A baby fox scurries across the road. A garden fire crackles; black vapours swirl upwards.

My hand meets the cold iron of my gate. It creaks open: it creaks shut. Footsteps down the path, the twigs of an overhanging tree brush against my face. They feel like the bones of a hand.

I stop and look around our front garden. Trousers twigged on the hawthorn; tattered ties and shorn socks on the grass. I gaze up at trousers floating, shirts parachuting and boxer shorts billowing in the breeze. They land on the lawn next to my football boots.

My football boots. My shirts. My ties. My clothes. Intruders in my house ransacking all my possessions. The Dog must be petrified. What if Shell is there?

I run into the building, charge up the stairs and burst through my unlocked front door.

There's no one in the bedroom or kitchen. Into the living room, roaring aggression, ready for everything they have. The Dog whimpers under the couch. A single figure crouches in middle of the room. Spinning round, she faces me, a knife in her hand, shredded clothes at her feet.

Shell.

She'd been here when they did it. Poor Shell, her jet black hair straggled, her face red with fury at what they'd done to our things.

'Where are they?' I say, my head rocketing from side to side, taking in the whirlwind of destruction, the rips in the curtains, the overturned furniture.

'Where are who?' she wails, the carving knife glinting in her hand.

'The people that did this.'

'It was me!'

'What was you?'

'All of it,' she yells, lurching forward and clawing the knife through a mound of my clothes.

I run to her and grab her arm. She wrestles herself free but I force both my arms under her arm pits and lock my hands behind her head. I hold her in this full nelson position but she flails wildly and we fall to the floor. The knife clatters across the room. She digs her heel into my shin, frees herself and scampers towards the blade. She lifts it from the floor.

'Shell, put it down!'

'DON'T YOU EVER HURT MY FRIENDS AGAIN. HOW DARE YOU ACCUSE ME OF BEING A SLUT AND SLEEPING WITH SPARKY.'

Her eyes cross as she stares at the point of the knife. She slowly rises from her knees to her feet.

I hold up my hands and walk towards her and say, 'Put. The knife. Down.'

She backs away, her hand twitching as she grips the

handle. 'STOP.'

I take another step. 'Put it down.'

'NO,' she yells, her arm drawing behind her head. She throws the knife. A silver blur. I shut my eyes. A stream of air passing my ear.

I turn and see the blade sunk into the sofa behind, its shaft pointing back toward me.

A murderous shriek. A body collides against mine and we fall to the ground. My mouth touches her cheek, the taste of salt, the scent of hatred. She grips my neck and presses her thumbs into my thorax. Her legs trap my arms. The only part of my body I can leverage is my feet. Blood in my eyes: death in hers. I gasp and somehow draw enough air to snatch a breath and kick with my legs and thrust upwards. I propel Shell off me and position myself between her and the knife still stuck in the couch.

We crouch and face each other.

Nothing in her eyes as she looks at me. The tantrum in the restaurant. Micky's words at the party, 'She's going to flip one day and try to kill someone. It'll probably be you.' The anarchist in London. The girl with the knife.

She tramples through the remains of my possessions and leaves the room, the house and maybe my life.

DAY 10

'Heard yer got chucked by your missus, Zezva,' Matty said, the moment I got on the team coach at football. Why had I told Micky the news? As if he could keep his big mouth shut.

'Well you heard wrong, didn't you,' I said, taking the only remaining seat across the aisle from Matty.

'I think I know why she dumped you. Johnny, tell him what a clit is,' Matty said.

'Isn't it a part of the vagina about the size of your brain, Matty,' I shot back, before Johnny's mouth even flinched.

'Oohhhh, don't getcha knickers in a knot,' Matty said.

'Anyway I chucked her,' I said.

'As if.'

'Too good for her. She did well to get me in the first place.'

'Bullshit, I heard she was having it away with another geezer,' Matty said.

'No wonder you couldn't satisfy her. The amount of hair down there on that hippy. You probably couldn't see a thing, mate,' Johnny said, grinning and excitedly nudging Matty with his elbow.

I opened my newspaper and folded it in two. 'Getting a bit jealous, Matty?'

'What's that supposed to mean?'

'Oh nothing.' I said, scanning the back page. 'Just all

this talk of hair.'

'I ain't going bald,' Matty said, running his hand over the top of his head.

'Nah, of course you ain't,' I said, mimicking his old school London accent. 'But remember, I can get another girlfriend Matty boy but there is something leaving you that is never coming back.'

'Fuck off,' Matty said but he was smiling at me.

And on the banter went, the same topics as usual but the tone had changed. You see I'd realised the mistake I was making with them. Before, I was trying to make them like me by being nice when the only way to impress such people was to be exactly like them: a grade A arsehole.

*

The traffic was terrible and we pulled into the ground only half an hour before kick off. We hurried off the bus, into the clubhouse and down to a changing room located in the basement. The room was about twelve by ten and barely six feet high. It had one solitary bench and a few broken hooks. Despite its size the most memorable feature was the smell; landlocked and windowless it hadn't tasted fresh air in all its rot filled days.

'They've put us in here on purpose to put us off,' Micky said. 'Oldest trick in the book.'

'Well, don't let it work. Come on lads, stop doing a Zezva and sitting there whinging. Get your heads up, get out there and get on with it,' the Gaffer said, his words inspirational to everyone. Everyone except me.

We got changed and then headed out to the pitch for a brief warm up and a hit of oxygen. A few stretches, a quick huddle and we were ready to kick off. The game was a qualifier for the FA Cup, which semi-professional teams throughout the country dream of playing in. With Nico out for months with his injury, the Gaffer had no choice but to start with me, despite our argument after the previous match.

Right from the kick off, I was back on my game; my dribbling was incisive, tackling sharp and passing accurate.

The game was tightly contested, played in good spirit, on the last hot day of the summer. The seven hundred or so spectators warmed to our efforts as they basked in the late August sun. We'd brought a decent amount of fans, with many of the regulars having made the journey across the Capital.

As the game continued, both teams missed numerous chances. We both rode our luck, taking it in turns to hit woodwork. I thought we were going out of the tournament when they won a penalty in the last few minutes of the second half, only for our Tunisian goalkeeper Sami to tip it round the post.

The final minute arrived and despite the abundance of goal-scoring opportunities the game was nil-nil. A replay at our home ground appeared inevitable.

With seconds left Matty intercepted an attempted clearance and made an uncharacteristic surge forward. He skipped past a player, showing a deftness of touch previously absent from his footballing, as well as social, repertoire. Perhaps surprising himself with this uncharacteristic display of skill, he drove towards goal. All of thirty-five yards out, the opposition were slow to close him down, almost inviting the cumbersome defender to try his luck. Never one to shirk a challenge, Matty swung his right boot. The ball sprung from his laces, its trajectory gradually rising, straight and undeviating. The goalkeeper was rooted to the spot as a microsecond later the ball thundered into the top corner of the net.

I leapt in astonishment and chased after Matty, running off the adrenaline surging through my body. I reached the mass of bodies piled on the grass and dived into the midst - the indescribable joy of eleven people achieving a common purpose.

Before our opponents had a chance to kick off the final whistle blew. I could see George dancing an arthritic jig on the sidelines. Ethel hobbled down the touchline, walking stick waving in the air. She launched herself into George's arms, kissing and hugging him like they were twenty one all over again.

After shaking the hands of the opposition with the warmth and sportsmanship that victory brings, I jogged back to the changing room, patting Matty on the back on the way, 'Great goal big man.'

'See that mug's face in the other team? That bastard was kicking me all game. That shut him up, dint it?' he said, expressing his joy through increased levels of aggression.

Round the changing room spun. Loud we sang. Drenched with beer. Whoever said team spirit was an illusion glimpsed in the aftermath of victory, had obviously had their arms around the Johnny or Matty of their team after such a victory. But at that instant I loved them, I really did. It was moments of such mind-bending irrationality that made me play in the first place.

*

We staggered off the bus, after celebrating the whole

way home. My cheeks burned with fatigue from the grin that was etched across my face.

I get deliriously happy when I drink and think I love everyone and that life isn't that bad and all I need is one more drink. At the start it makes me the person I want to be. At the end it makes me the person I fear I've become. When I have too much the pendulum swings and I wake up the next day and feel hungover and cheated that my joy was a drunken sham.

So I don't drink much, which is why when the other players headed away to celebrate, Micky and I left. Micky wasn't going out with the rest of team because he thought large groups of men would affect his chances of getting in clubs, which would in turn affect his chances of pulling.

'That Matty's a pure bam but that goal was a belter,' Micky said.

'It made me like him for about an hour, so it must have been a good goal.'

'I like the way you're telling them both to get themselves to fuck now. I cannae believe the amount of abuse that you've taken fae them without snapping. To be honest with you, it's aboot time ye grew some baws. Is that what happened to make Shell dump you?'

'Not exactly.'

'What happened?'

'She smashed up my things and tried to knife me.'

'Lassies, eh?' Micky said with a shrug.

'What do you mean "lassies, eh?" How many times has a woman tried to kill you?'

'Hundreds of times.'

'Listen, I'm being serious!'

'Really?'

'Yes, she threw a knife at me and tried to strangle me.'

'I was wondering why you looked like you've been shaving with a rake.' Micky said, peering at my neck. 'How comes she did that?'

'No reason at all,' I said, which was stretching the truth a bit but...

'Unbe-fucking-lievable. I telt you at that party that she wasnae all there in the heid,' he said, boring his finger into the centre of his forehead. 'I tell you what but.... she's gone up massively ma estimations. Do you want her like a hundred times more the now?'

'Of course I don't. I want her a hundred times less.'

'That's a real turn on for me. I love they wee rockets,' Micky shook his shaved head with adoring respect. 'Bet she was a real handful in bed.'

As I walked down the street with him, I became worried that I was completely literate in Micky logic. Her edge was what made her lustful and dangerous. What did that say about me that I'd liked that?

'Right now you're single, and acting like a man for the first time, let's celebrate by going out and getting ourselves some women. I'll be your wing man.'

'You wouldn't be though, would you? You'd just pass the ugly mates to me.'

'You're actually no a bad looking guy. If you could just hold it together for once I reckon we'd be some team.'

'We'll see...'

He threw his arm over my shoulder with such affection he almost knocked me over, 'Is that an aye then?'

*

It was an aye.

We sat on Micky's cream, wipe-clean sofa having a beer.

Micky finished his bottle and said, 'Right here's the plan. Get changed, have another drink, discuss tactics and then out to the dancing.'

'Discuss tactics? We aren't playing Manchester United?'

'Now you're single you cannae keep acting like you do. There's no way you're ready to go out on the pull. It's a jungle out there. You'll embarrass yourself or even worse you'll embarrass me.'

I tipped my bottle towards him. 'Cheers... at least I feel confident now.'

'For starters we need to gee you a character. Right, first thing that needs to be done is to change your name.'

'What is wrong with my name?'

Micky looked me dead in the eyes and his expression was regretful but sincere as he delivered the following necessary truth. 'Ye know how some things will always set you off badly with a lassie like having cold sores or spots? Well your name is the same. Naebody cool has ever been called Zezva. Ever. As soon as you introduce yourself you've already blown it with that name and your clothes. And it's no as if you have a chance of recovering it with your patter. That's how ye end up with pure scowlers like Shell smashing up your tatty auld furniture.'

He sat back and stroked his chin. He began to click his fingers and wince.

'What are you doing?' I said.

'Trying to think of a new name for you.'

'Is thinking of a name really that hard for you?'

Ignoring me, he leant forward and gripped his head and muttered to himself, 'Come on, concentrate.' He was really getting into his new altruistic persona. Like many philanthropists Micky was a very privileged man himself, who recognised his good luck, and wanted to give something back to those who were considerably less fortunate than himself: people like me.

He let go off his hair and clicked his fingers, 'That's it. You should call yourself Ricky or Dicky.'

'So basically I should have a name that rhymes with yours?'

'Aye, exactly,' he said with a precise nod. 'Next on the list is your clobber. Right you've said Shell cut up all your clothes so I won't have a go at you about what you're wearing the night,' he said, pointing at my best pair of jeans and shirt.

I'd felt so relieved when Shell hadn't cut them up.

'It doesnae matter anyhow. As I says, it's no your fault,' said Micky, misinterpreting my chagrin. 'You can wear something of mine.'

'Who are we going out with anyway?'

'Ma man Colin.'

'There is absolutely no way I'm going out with him.'

'How no?'

'The small matter of him being potentially sociopathic.'

'So having great patter and looking great makes you a bad guy in your book. Aye that explains a lot. You should watch and learn off this character. He absolutely cleans up with the women,' said Micky, using the only category of character judgment he knew.

*

Micky spent an hour or so getting ready: trimming his beard and hair to the exact same lengths; making sure his chain and watch matched his earring; stretching his new t-shirt at the neck to make it look worn; moisturising; deodorising; plucking.

Bored by what was probably now considered to be modern masculinity, I drank through the tedious wait. After a final long, loving stare in the mirror, he was ready to leave. Once outside we hailed a taxi and headed into town to meet the C word.

The bar was packed by the time we arrived, which coincided with the pre-club rush. Breaking through the hub of activity, we saw Colin standing at the back of the room. Micky's friend had deep set eyes, a crooked nose and brown tanned skin. His hair was over-gelled and spiked upwards. He leaned on the bar chomping on his gum in that way cocky people do: smacking his lips with a curl of the eyebrow.

As Micky got the pints in, I was left in the company of Colin. 'Been scrapping have you my man?' he said, pointing at my various injuries: lumped forehead, black eye and scratched neck, etc. 'What does the other guy look like?'

He had a strong accent but pronounced every letter in every word – he spoke like Micky but with fewer short cuts. In a strange way it made him even less charming.

'No, just football injuries,' I lied.

'Aye no bother. To tell you the truth I say the same thing when I've taken a doing. The thing is it doesn't matter, we've all been there.'

His pats on the back felt more like thumps. I realised I needed to change the subject – if only to stop him touching me. 'So Colin what are you doing down here?'

'As you know yourself, I'm in the army but I'm off for a wee while.'

'How did you get into that again?' I said, glancing to the bar, hoping Micky would return to save me from the answer.

'I've always been rock hard. It's kind of my thing. Ask Micky what I was like at school, by the way. I was off my head, so I was. So the army was the best place for me,' he said, puffing out his pigeon chest. 'Just finished a tour last week actually, but. Got some mint stories. I mind this day when we were doing a patrol and out of nowhere there were hundreds of guys shooting at us.'

'Hundreds?'

'Aye. There was only about four of us. Still fucked them up but,' he said. 'Anyhow, one of our guys got shot. I was out there straight away. Dillions of bullets flying past us. Did this commando roll, grabbed him and took him into cover. Just before he died, he looked at us, right into my eyes and says "Nick, I've –"'

'Nick? What did he call you that for?'

'He always did, the wee prick. He couldn't get my name right,' he said, even managing to scratch his own head aggressively. 'But the message was the same. I was the bravest man he'd met.'

'Are you sure he didn't mean another guy called Nick?

'Nah, he knew my rep.'

'But not your name?'

'Nah no my name,' Colin said, not a flicker of doubt passing across his brainless countenance. 'It's a scandal that I've not won a medal for it.'

'Well at least you've got a true story to tell people in pubs,' I consoled.

'Aye, there is that,' he said, taking his pint from the returning Micky.

'Right troops I'm off to powder my nose.' He winked and swaggered away.

I turned to Micky. 'What's he on about? Powder his nose.'

'Jesus Christ what do you think?'

I watched Colin going into the men's. 'I should have known you need substances to be like him.'

'How?'

'It's not naturally possible to be that much of a bellend.'

'You said that you werenae gonna moan about Colin.' Micky glared at me. I could tell he was already regretting asking me along.

'Fine but don't leave me talking to him again. Why does he need to go on about the army all the time?'

'Show some respect - that guy is risking his life for us.'

'I doubt he's risking his life. And if he is, he's doing it for the stories and for some American corporations. Not me.'

Micky laughed. 'You sound like that lassie of yours.'

'Never say that again.' I slammed my pint down on the bar; a white fountain of beer frothing over the edge of the glass. A woman put her hand on her chest bone in shock and glared at us.

Micky held his hand up in apology and hissed at me out of the corner of his mouth. 'Stop embarrassing us. You fucking heid case.'

'You hang around with Colin and you're calling me a –'

'What you saying about me?' Colin said, returning from the toilet rubbing his nose with the back of his hand.

'Nothing,' I mumbled into my beer.

'Thought I heard my name.'

'Not your name Colin,' I said. 'No, we were talking

about a guy called Nick.'

'No you and all. My name isn't Nick!'

'Exactly. So how could we be talking about you?'

'You couldn't, I suppose....' Colin frowned. 'Right, I'm off to play the puggies.'

I watched him sloping off to the nearest fruit machine and said to Micky, 'Lucky he's so daft or that could have been embarrassing.'

Micky looked at me quizzically, 'Who's Nick?'

*

When we finished our drinks, we made the short walk to the nearby club and joined the back of a queue.

Fifteen minutes of foot-tapping, arm-folding and fidgeting later and we were still nowhere near the front. The bouncers smugly nodded to each other as female after female strolled to the front and went inside. The final insult was when a girl walked to the front of the line eating a burger and was let straight in.

'I'm gonee go up and talk to them,' Micky said. 'I know some people round here. Come on Colin. Zezva, you stay here. We don't want you fucking it.'

When they left I didn't bother to check their progress. Instead I stared at my feet praying that the rowdy group of girls behind didn't make the mistake of thinking that talking to me would improve their night. Hearing a shrill whistle from the front, I looked up to see the unexpected sight of Micky beckoning me towards him and inside.

*

A grimy beat licked around the packed room. We

squeezed ourselves through the walls of perfume, past groups of girls surrounded by lads wearing shirts and gormless expressions.

The room was fevered, dirty, thrilling, disgusting. Time for the hibernation of morality; the lowering of inhibitions; living for the love of that moment and the next. Pretty soon they would be fighting, shagging, crying, munching kebabs, arguing with their best friends – in some cases all at the same time. They'd feel terrible about it the next day: they'd do it all again the next week.

I lingered next to Colin and Micky, who were leaning against the bar, trying to look like they could take or leave the place. 'There,' Colin said, urgently gesturing with his head.

And they were gone. Sitting down next to a group of girls. Before I could blink.

This is what I was competing against now I was single. I didn't notice the opening and it was already filled. The girls were great looking and even worse they seemed to be warming to the womanising duo; giggling, whispering in each others' ears, giving knowing looks to the two sharkers. They obviously weren't very good judges of character but to be fair to them the music was very loud.

It was then that I decided to drink into oblivion. Three doubles later, still bored, still standing alone watching the two master sleazes at work, I decided to sit next Micky. He predictably ignored me. After twenty minutes of nodding my head to the music, looking at my phone and various other techniques to avoid appearing like a complete loner, I gave up.

'Micky, I'm dying here,' I said, finally getting his attention after numerous prods.

'Don't worry, they've got some friends coming in a minute,' he reassured.

On cue two girls arrived and greeted their friends with over the top kisses. Listen, I'm probably the last person who should be critical of the way other people look but I couldn't work out how these two sets of girls knew each other: perhaps the two seated beauties were models on a night out with their assistants. When the assistants sat down next to me, again I don't want to be rude, so let's just say it was a tight fit and leave it at that.

'Long queue outside?' I said, practising talking to women while the pressure was off.

'No, we just walked straight in,' the one next to me replied. The burger trick had obviously worked again.

We chatted away for a while, and it was pleasant enough, but they appeared as unimpressed with me as I was with them. It was the classic scenario where two sets of people thought they were too good for the other and both had a point. Stalemate ensued. I had to get out of there. I shouted in Micky's ear, 'Right, I'm going for a wander.'

'Why? This is magic.' He faced me but his fingers rested on his girl's shoulder, playing with the strap on her slinky black dress.

'Magic for you maybe but I'm stuck over here with these two.'

'You mean they are stuck with you.'

'Swap then.'

'Nae chance!'

'Exactly,' I said. 'Where's Colin?'

'He's gone with that lassie.'

'Gone where?'

'Home. The guy's a champion. It makes you proud to know him.'

At the time I thought that news summed up everything that was wrong with the world.

To everyone's relief, I excused myself and got up and walked through the club. As the floor sloped to the right, the walls swayed to the left, I was sure of only one thing: I was drunk.

I staggered past the dance floor towards the toilets.

On entering the gents I was greeted by the toilet attendant bellowing, 'Fresh, fresh, frrreeessshhh up.' With no other option, I followed the noise to the sinks and turned on the tap. The attendant took this move as a personal affront and started to wash my hands for me. Despite my best attempts to shrug him off he was now drying my hands and straightening my collar. Seeing no other escape, I chucked a pound into his jar. Rather than get rid of him, this sent him into over-drive. He offered me condoms, deodorants, lollipops, mints whilst massaging the tension in my shoulders that, ironically, was being created by his attention. Eventually, realising he'd done well to get a pound out of me, he gave up and attacked another unsuspecting male whilst spraying aftershave and shrieking his catch phrase, 'Fresh, fresh, frrreeessshhh up.' The poor man had the worst job and the most enthusiasm; life was so unfair.

Released from his attention, I splashed water on my face, the cold liquid sending a revitalising chill through my body. Before I could repeat the act I felt a tapping on my shoulder. I turned around and was faced with a large, bald man dressed in black. He wore an ear piece and uncompromising expression.

'Right sir, I'll need to search you,' he said. Why was he calling me sir like he was providing me with a service?

'No point, you have me bang to rights,' I said, putting my hands up in surrender. 'I was washing my face.'

'Right smart arse. That's it you're gone,' he said, adding himself to the already extensive list of people who didn't appreciate my attempts at humour.

He twisted my arm behind my back, marched me out the toilets and used my body as a battering ram as we barged through some swing doors into a corridor. The music faded leaving only the dull thud of the base.

'What are you doing?' I shouted over my shoulder.

'I'm throwing you out.'

'If you wanted to punish me, you should keep me in this shit tip,' I yelled.

He didn't seem to agree. He opened the back door and chucked me into the outside lane like a sack of garbage. I lay on the cobbles and moss and who knows what else. The doors slammed shut.

*

I sat on the kerb on the main road, surrounded by the swaying rowdiness of an early Sunday morning. I could smell kebab meat, sewage, sick, diesel fumes, tension.

I was considering leaving Micky and going home when two high-heeled shoes clipped to a halt next to me. They were attached to a pair of long legs, covered by a black dress slit to the upper thigh. Those legs bent and a woman sat next to me on the kerb. Long, loose strands of brown hair cascaded onto her shoulders framing her face.

'Are you Micky's friend?' she said.

I nodded.

'I was the girl talking to him inside,' she said, making the mistake of thinking that a man would see her and forget about it. 'He's really cocky, isn't he?'

I couldn't be bothered lying so I said, 'Yes, he is.'

She sighed, 'Most men are.'

'They aren't. It's just that you don't get a realistic sample.'

Her blue eyes sparkled with interest. 'What do you mean?'

'It's because you're good-looking. The only guys who talk to you are cocky or putting on a false bravado. The normal ones don't approach because they are too scared to talk to you. The result is that you think all men are cocky.'

'Maybe you're right.' She gave me that look that women do when they finally meet someone that understands. 'Why are you out here anyway?

'I was thrown out.'

'What for?'

'The bouncer's ego'

She smiled and somehow her face managed to become even more gorgeous when animated.

'Anyway, why are you out here?' I said. 'I thought you were getting on well with Micky.'

'He's pretty immature and stupid.'

'He is actually quite a nice guy in his own way. His friend Colin, who left with your friend... now that's a different story.'

'She didn't leave with him! She left early and he followed her all the way to the taxi.'

'You probably should check she got home OK. He's bad news.'

'Aren't you nice?' she said, giving me a playful punch.

'She messaged me: she's fine.'

I breathed out and felt genuine relief – which didn't say a lot for the company I was keeping in those days.

'It was so annoying inside,' she said. 'I wanted to talk to you not them. You're definitely the cutest.'

I furrowed my eyebrows and gave a mini shrug - pretending that I was the type of person who such things were said about all the time.

'You seem really smart too,' she said.

If I didn't know better I would have thought this unbelievably attractive woman was coming onto me.

'Thanks. Easy audience I think.'

'Are you calling me easy?'

'No of course not,' I said, petrified I'd offended this stunning stranger.

'Well I am.' She tilted her head and flapped her eyes lashes in feigning prissiness. 'With the right man of course.'

I swallowed and averted my eyes. Was I meant to suggest that I could be that man? Was the fact that she was flagging down a taxi a sign that the moment had passed?

A black cab pulled up and she got up and inside. Still I'd given no response. She wound down the window and viewed me wallowing in my own stupidity.

'Are you not getting in?' she said.

'Me?' I said, pointing to myself.

Perhaps reasoning that it was impossible for anyone to be so uncool, she presumed I was joking and said, 'OK, I know what you're doing. Stop playing and get inside.'

I sprung to my feet and hastened towards the cab before she changed her mind.

DAY 11

I knew it was going to be a bad day the moment I awoke and dreaded opening my eyes. Disorientated and in excruciating pain, my body was contorted like I'd been trying to perform a headstand in my sleep. Disentangling my limbs, I groaned as my joints snapped back into place. Other than the minor spinal damage my body was fine; the worst of the malaise was taking place in my head. A chainsaw droning in my ears; my mouth feeling like a tumbler of salt had been emptied into it; my tongue like it had been grated. If I'd woken up feeling that bad and hadn't been drinking, I'd have gone straight to hospital. Worst of all I was naked and alone; a terrible combination when you don't know where you are.

I hauled myself up, shivering despite the heat of the stuffy room. I took ten deep breaths, counting each one whilst murmuring, 'Don't be sick.'

Reaching a nauseous equilibrium, I began to study the murky surroundings. I was facing a pine dressing table, its surface littered with bottles and cases, appliers and removers, straighteners and curlers. An empty bookcase to its right; a gigantic wardrobe to the left, an open door revealing tens of dresses - green, red, white, black, blue, slit, short, strapless.

I averted my eyes to the floor. My socks were resting on a red bra, flanked by my boxer shorts, next to some crumpled jeans and a black dress.

The bedroom door opened and a naked woman strode into the room. 'Morning!'

I sat bolt upright. 'Hello.'

She walked to the curtains, opened them and studied the street below. And there she stood, still unclothed, putting on a show for the world. She certainly had tremendous body confidence. Looking at her I could see why.

Deciding she'd given her pervy neighbours their fill for the day, she walked over to the bed and perched on the edge. She arched her back and pushed her chest forward like I should speak to her breasts rather than her face and said. 'I had a great time last night.'

'Thank you,' I said – because I'm default polite when I can't think of anything else to say.

I imagine these moments are pretty uncomfortable for even past masters like Micky. For me they are excruciating.

I sprung up out of the bed. My legs swayed unable to support my weight: I was still drunk.

'What are you doing?' she said

I began gathering my clothes, 'Getting dressed.'

'Are you sure you want to do that? Last night was so much fun...'

'Was it?'

'Yes.' She approached as I was hopping into my boxer shorts and slapped my bum and rasped in my ear. 'It felt so good without a condom. It's sending tingles down my spine thinking about it.'

I yanked my boxer shorts up and laughed one of those laughs where you're definitely not laughing inside. 'The thing is that's a good joke but...' I did another one of those laughs / non laughs. 'I'd never be that stupid.'

She flicked her hair back which made her blue eyes more prominent and enticing. 'You were.'

'I don't recall anything like that.'

She giggled and then kissed me on the lips, 'Does that help your memory?'

Unfortunately it did and that was when I knew that she was telling the truth.

'I have to go,' I garbled and continued to put on the rest of my clothes. In my condition that wasn't as easy as it sounds. When I'd completed the task I checked my pockets for the wallet, phone, keys combo and was ready to leave.

'Shall I leave my phone number?' I said, unsure of the appropriate etiquette.

'Are we going to see each other again?'

'I'm not sure.'

'Of course we aren't,' she said, flashing her pearly white teeth. 'Don't look so worried. You don't have to take me on a date.'

'You won't think I've used you?' I said.

That really made her laugh. After a while she got herself under control and said, 'You've not had a one night stand before have you?'

'I've had loads.'

'You're a rubbish liar. But a very cute one.'

'Thank you. I should go.' I kissed her on the cheek,

dodged out of the room and jogged down the stairs to the front door. I jerked the handle. It didn't move. Locked in and panicking, I started to rattle it hysterically. I felt a tap on the shoulder.

'You will need these,' the girl said, dangling a set of keys in front of my face. She was still naked. Still casual. How many times had she done this? She brushed past me and opened the door almost reluctantly.

I hurried out and met a road like most others in London: terraced houses below a grey sky. I walked to the left, pretending to know where I was going and where I'd been. I rounded the corner and broke into a canter that turned into a jog that developed into a sprint. A booted man in a shirt, pelting though the streets on a Sunday morning. Through the windy morning I went, alcohol streaming from my eyes, my feet thudding on the pavement. I ran on, harder and faster, but it wouldn't go away. None of it.

A bus passed and exhaled its effluent. I sucked the diesel fumes deep into my lungs and spluttered and thought I was going to be sick and had to stop. I put my hands on my knees and panted and realised that although most people ran away from their problems that they didn't try to do it literally.

Feeling ridiculous, I took my phone out of my pocket. I needed to talk to someone. Someone that knew about these things.

*

I entered the cafe and passed the kitchen. Two women in blue aprons slaved away, gloveless hands wiping the sweat away from hatless heads. Frying pans spat; milk frothed over pans; ladles slopped porridge into chipped bowls.

Nobody looked up from their plates as I wove between the tables to Micky sitting at the window. In front of him sat a mash of beans, bread and eggs; a plate that looked like it had been gnawed by a vagrant dog. He cheered and got to his feet.

'Here comes the mad shagger. You've no idea how much you've gone up in ma estimations,' he said and hugged me.

It felt like his arms were squeezing my intestines. 'Get off. I feel sick,' I said, fighting him off me.

I sat down, moved a giant red tomato filled with ketchup of out the way and leaned on the plastic table cloth. 'What was that all about?'

'What?' Micky said, sitting down across from me.

'That's the first time you've hugged me. In fact, you didn't even hug me when my mum died.'

'I done it cos you pulled that amazing lassie.'

'How do you know?'

'I seen you getting in a taxi with her.'

I wet my lips with my tongue and looked him dead in his lively green eyes. 'Sorry.'

'How?'

'You were talking to her all night...'

'And?'

'You're not annoyed?'

'Course I'm no.' Micky began cleaning up his plate with something that looked like a piece of bread. 'Part of the game my man. I'm proud of you.'

A waitress approached and lingered behind Micky. She wiped her hands down her apron and waited for me to talk. But Micky, who was either ignoring her or had no idea she was behind him, was still going on, 'You know she's an actual glamour model. She's been in all the internet and everything. I cannae believe you got a lumber with her. You wee fucking machine you –'

I cleared my throat and said to the waitress, 'A coffee, please.'

'No food?' she said, looking at me like my lack of hunger was a personal affront.

'No, thank you.'

I waited until she left and said to Micky. 'Could you not have waited until she left?'

'She doesnae care. How comes you're no eating, anyhow?'

'I don't think I've ever felt this hungover.'

'Quit your greeting and tell us your story,' he said, wiggling on his plastic chair in anticipation. 'What were your moves on her?'

'She came onto me.'

'Nooo. She was hot! That never happened.'

'It did.'

'Hoor!' Micky shouted, overcome by a surge of misogynistic Tourette's. A tattooed man stopped dunking his sausage into his tea, some plasterers glared at us, two old women fell silent. I got to my feet to leave.

Micky grabbed my arm and dragged me back down. 'Where you going?'

'Why did you shout that? What the hell is wrong with you?' I hissed.

'Sorry I couldnae stop myself. I'm so pleased for you so I am. Must be losing my touch. Colin messaged me: he got his nuts an all.'

I didn't want to tell him Colin had gone home alone. It would be like proving to a Christian that Jesus was a myth; I didn't want to obliterate Micky's entire belief system.

'I feel so dirty,' I said, changing the subject. 'I want to get in a shower for a week.'

'Did you use a sheet?'

'Yes and a mattress as well.'

'A sheet as in a condom, daftie.'

'No.'

'You're kidding me on? She's one lassie you don't want to do that with. I'd have double bagged.'

'Stop it.'

'Seriously, the bets are off on whether she's got something, the question is what. If it's Gary Gonorrhoea or Clammy Chlamydia nae worries cos pills can get rid of it but if it's Harry Herpes that never goes away.'

'I can see you're the expert on this,' I said, through clenched teeth.

'Don't turn this onto me. You're the one that needs to get yourself down to the stick doctor.'

'Stick doctor?'

'Sexual Disease shop pal. You better hope they're no geeing away a two for one offer,'

'That won't be necessary.'

'It'll be shut today so get yourself down there the morrow.'

Thankfully my phone buzzed in my pocket. I took it out and saw a message from Liz. It said, "Where are you? Don't tell me you've forgotten! I have the tickets."

Tickets? I racked my brain and couldn't think what on earth she was talking about. It was probably something I'd agreed to go to without listening. I'd blag it when I got there. 'There in ten minutes,' I replied to Liz.

'Cancel my coffee, I've got to go,' I said to Micky, standing up too quickly, black spots splattering in front of my eyes.

'Why?'

'I'm going to meet Liz.'

'What? Her and all? You wee beauty ya.'

He was making gestures with his arms now... I bolted out the door, escaping the café and Micky.

Fortunately, Liz was only two stops away on the tube.

*

I dragged myself up the stairs, pressed the bell and waited. Click. The door opened ajar, held by a golden chain. A sigh later and Liz undid the latch. The door opened but there was no greeting. She was wearing jogging bottoms and a hooded top. Her hair was tied back, which I'd only seen her do when she played sport. As I became more confused about what these tickets could be for, she turned and limped into the kitchen.

I followed her. 'How did you hurt your leg? More judo?'

She sat down at the table and said in a quiet voice, 'No.'

I sat down across from her, pushed two empty bottles of wine and an unscrewed bottle of pain killers out of the way and rested my elbows on the surface.

The blinds were still drawn. Peering through the dim light, I searched for the cause of the stale smell.

'Why are you pulling that face?' she said.

I didn't want to mention that her kitchen smelt of rubbish and gone off food so I said, 'No reason... I was just wondering why we were sitting down.'

'Why not?'

I drummed my hands on the table. 'Don't we need to go?'

'Go where Zezva?'

'To the ticket thing.'

'You have no idea what the *ticket thing* is do you?'

I winced. 'Not entirely...'

'You told me months ago that you wanted to go. I bought them for your birthday. You said it was the best gift you could have received.'

I clenched my eyes shut and wracked my brain but the more I willed myself to remember the more my head hurt and I couldn't.

'Have you honestly forgotten?' she said. 'Do I mean that little to you?'

'Look I know it looks bad but I'm not myself at the moment.'

'How am I meant to know that when you don't talk to me?'

'I've not had a chance.'

'What about the answer phone message I left you? You didn't reply.'

A cold chill ran through my body. Her message after tennis. She'd sounded so upset. With all that had happened, I'd forgotten to call her back.

I stretched across the table and put my hand on hers. Her fingers felt freezing cold. 'I'm so sorry that I forgot. Some bad things have happened since I last saw you.'

'Like what?'

'Shell tried to kill me...'

'I don't really blame her,' she muttered.

Her response didn't really seem appropriate so I said, 'I

came home and she was trashing my things. When I tried to stop her she attacked me with a knife.'

'And what caused this scene?' Liz said. *Scene*. Could she trivialise it any further?

'Another *scene* at Sparky's house.'

She nodded and continued to stare absently out of her kitchen window with its view of nothing. Whatever I said no one would take this story as literal. I could walk around with a sign saying "SHELL TRIED TO KILL ME" and people would say, "My back is killing me" or "I could have murdered a Big Mac last night" or something like that.

I withdrew my hand from hers and pushed my seat back from the table.

She looked at me, her turquoise eyes big and angry. 'There is no point moving away now. I've already smelt the alcohol.'

'That's not why I was moving away from –'

'Why do you stink of booze at this time?'

'It's from last night.'

'What happened last night?'

I knew Liz was annoyed at me but her reaction to Shell's attempted murder had annoyed me. To be honest I still wasn't really over the Blackie thing either. So I told the truth. 'I went out and got drunk and had sex with a random girl.'

She glared at me and said almost in a shriek. 'Why are you telling me that?'

'Why wouldn't I?' I was goading her but wanted to know the response. 'I mean, that's what friends talk about, isn't it?'

'I can't believe you just burst in and announced that.'

'I didn't burst in and announce it. I walked in and then

183

you asked.'

'SHUT UP WITH YOUR SMART ARSE CORRECTIONS.'

I suppose I've had quite a lot of conflict in my life. Usually words like 'Shut up,' wouldn't even register. But when someone so polite raises their voice and says something like that it really has an impact. But she hadn't finished.

'And to think you made me feel terrible about that one kiss with Blackie. Something I regret so much. Something I've been worrying about all week. You're the most self-centred, arrogant, unaware wanker I've ever met.'

Had she just called me a wanker? It was all so out of character, however much I deserved it. I looked at her – I mean properly. Then things began to drop into place. 'You're annoyed we aren't going to this ticket thing but you aren't even dressed.' I looked around the kitchen. 'I thought you were house proud. It's disgusting in here.'

'Are you really having a go at me?'

'No, I just want to know what's happening with you?'

She laughed and clapped her hands hysterically. 'Did you actually ask me how I was?'

'Why is that so funny?'

'Because you don't care about me or my problems. All you care about is yourself.'

'What problems? You don't have any problems.'

'Exactly! That's what you think. Do you know what you have turned into? The person you used to hate. Worst of all you trample over the only person who truly loves you.'

'Who?'

'Shell,' she said, almost in a wail. 'Yes! Shell! That's who

I was talking about,'

'Have you been listening to me? Shell tried to ki –'

'GGGGEEEETTT OOOOUUUTT,' she screamed.

I sat stunned.

'YOU HEARD ME GET OUT. I'M NOT TAKING THIS ANYMORE. NOT FROM MATTY, NOT FROM THE PEOPLE AT WORK AND ESPECIALLY NOT FROM YOU.'

I got up and looked at her and it was the revulsion in her face as much as the shouting that made me realise I had to leave.

In the chaos of my life, she was the one person I didn't need to worry about. I took her for granted because she was constant, reliable, there.

But she wasn't. Not forever. No one is.

Things had moved and I'd stood still.

I sat on the tube on the way home and thought about Liz. I wished I'd returned her call and asked her what was wrong. I wished I'd remembered the tickets. I wished I hadn't told her about that girl. But most of all I wished Liz wasn't with Matty so I could go back to her house and tell her she was the only reason that I lived and she was the most beautiful, kind person I'd ever met and I was so sorry, for today, for every day and for everything.

DAY 12

I sat at my desk at work and read various health websites. I couldn't grip the mouse; my eyes flitted across the monitor; my fingers quivered as they tapped on the keyboard. The hypochondria of web diagnosis had already set in.

Accepting that the girl from the club had laden me with every sexual disease going, I specialised my knowledge, branching out to neurology, cardiology, oncology. My kidneys ached, my legs felt numb, joints stiff, eyes burned. I was a dyslexic, depressive, diabetic, AIDS sufferer with an overactive thyroid. I had polio, TB, HIV, rickets and ADD.

On the cusp of fainting, I sensed a shadow behind my desk. Minimising the page, to avoid office gossip that I was suffering from tuberculosis, I could tell by the dense must of perfume that it was my secretary, Jayne, who was lingering. I swivelled in my chair to face her.

'What are you doing?' she said.

'What do you mean?' I croaked through the cancerous lump in my throat.

'You're pale, you're soaked with sweat and your hand is shaking,' she said, more disgusted than concerned.

'You would be if you had to smell your perfume,' I

said.

'What did you say?'

'I said that I liked your perfume,' I said.

'Oh right...'she said, her expression morphing from grave to quite pleased.

'Right listen, I need to go out for a bit.' I locked my computer, stood up and picked up my jacket. 'If anyone asks I've gone to the optician. No, in fact say the dentist, that's better.'

Her face was grave again. 'Are you going to the dentist or the optician?'

'Neither. But I want you to tell anyone that asks that I'm going to the dentist.'

'OK,' she said, raising her drawn-on eyebrows. 'How long will you be gone for?'

'Just say to anyone who asks, "Oh, that's unlucky you just missed him," however long I've been away.'

'Well if that's what you want me to do, that's what I'll do. I'm sure you'll be very grateful,' she folded her arms even tighter and added, 'as usual.'

*

When I was a safe distance away from the office I stole down a side alley and took out my phone. I had no idea what to do but knew someone who would.

'Hi, it's me. Listen, I've been thinking about what you said and think I should go to the sex disease doctor man.'

'Ah I knew you would crack and end up going. What symptoms have you got?'

'The symptoms of most major illnesses.'

'When did they start?'

'After I slept with that girl and started reading the

187

internet.'

'You havenae got nothing bad. Put it this way: it's no a VD RIP situation. All she's given you is basic nut rot. Get yourself down to the rot doc and the joab's a good un.'

'Where's the nearest one to here?'

'What's your current postcode?'

'Central London.'

'St Bart's then.'

'What are you, a fucking STD GPS?'

'St Bart's is no a bad one either. I like it myself. It's quite efficient. No as good as Enfield but few are. Whatever ye do, don't ever go to Knightsbridge. I came out of there with more than I went in with.'

'Is it horrible?'

'It's no exactly a day out at Alton Towers but you'll live. I tell you what actually. I'm no doing nothing this morning and I'm near St Bart's. I need to get checked up and all. I've been doing some damage recently. I'll pop doon and gee you some moral support.'

'Sure, Micky, I'll meet you there. Wear a red scarf.'

'Sorted.'

I was sure he was joking but couldn't risk it. I hung up instantly. Desperate to get checked out before Micky arrived, I started waving my arms at any passing car. At last one turned out to be a taxi.

It took me right to the main entrance. I paid and got out and entered into a packed waiting room. I walked to the front desk, which was manned by a receptionist seated behind a glass window. Head bowed, she flicked through a file.

'Excuse me.'

'Please take a number from the dispenser and you'll be

seen shortly.'

'I don't want to be seen. I want directions.'

She put down the file and glared at me like I'd asked her to drive me to Inverness. 'Go on then.'

'Where is the STD clinic, please?' I said, the sound barely permeating the air outside my mouth.

'Sorry I can't hear you?' she shouted into the microphone. Two elderly patients in the front row lurched, petrified by the sheer volume of her voice.

'Can you tell me where the STD clinic is please?' I whispered.

'It's not called that. It's called the Genitourinary Medicine clinic or GUM.'

'I'm sure the whole waiting room found that fascinating.' I lowered my voice. 'Could you tell me where it is please? Quietly.'

'The GUM clinic is through the doors, down the corridor and on your left,' she bellowed, mapping my route out with over-the-top arm gestures, in case I didn't know what *left* meant.

I shielded my face, hurried out the waiting room and walked down a corridor, the odours of sick, bleach and formaldehyde amalgamating into a concoction of aromatic misery.

Arriving at the clinic, the mere sight of the GUM placard sent a shot of pain through my groin. There were two doors, one marked male: the other female. I sneaked inside to find a desk staffed by a woman. She slipped me a piece of paper without eye contact or saying a word.

This was more like it.

It had a personal details section and at the bottom a checklist of illnesses you could be tested for. They included things the internet hadn't alerted me to. One possibility was a test for crabs. I had no idea what this was but was sure the person that discovered this disorder could have thought of a nicer name. I ticked all options and went to sit in the cosily arranged group of seats filled with men and nasty diseases.

I sat down and picked up a magazine that was three years old. I'd never read anything as dull but concentrated on it like it was an exam paper as I tried to block out the rest of the waiting room. A guy with headphones on clicked to a beat no one else could hear. Another patient slammed his foot down every five seconds like he was complaining to a noisy neighbour below. Someone coughed liked they were gulping down helium.

For an hour, I sat in there, staring at that rock climbing magazine, trying to ignore the tapping, clicking and coughing.

Then all of a sudden I heard. 'You alright, doll? I've no seen you in a while.'

I froze. He'd actually come.

'Hi Micky,' the previously mute receptionist said. 'How are you?'

'No bad,' he said, taking off a red scarf. 'Good to see ye again. I don't need the form, just the usual please.'

I hid behind the magazine but it didn't work. The sound of bounding steps, a body sitting next to me, 'Alright, how's it going –'

I dug my elbow into his ribs and moved up a seat. 'Don't talk to me,' I said out of the corner of my mouth.

At that moment a man came out of one of the two examination rooms. He walked across the room and sat between me and Micky. He had a pleasant face, delicate blue eyes and thin brown hair parted down the middle. Despite his vicar-like looks all I could think was what nasty venereal disease does he have? It appeared I was soon going to find out - he was twitching and trying to make eye contact in that way people do when they want to spark up a conversation.

'Have you been in yet?' he said, realising my worst nightmare and actually conversing with me.

'Not yet.'

'You're in for a shock, mate. It really stings.'

Why was he talking to me like we were in the post office? I couldn't think of anything else to say but, 'Does it.'

He took this statement as a question and said, 'Yes it does.'

'Too right,' Micky said, desperate to join in the worst conversation I'd participated in. 'So what were you having done?' he asked the man.

Before this stranger could reveal the intimate details of his experience, a nurse called out my name.

I sprung up and practically sprinted towards her.

'Wait for us in that square outside,' Micky called after me.

I nodded and followed the nurse to a nearby room, leaving Micky and the stranger deep in conversation.

The nurse paused outside the door. She was a large forearmed, short-legged woman with a kind, red face. 'Hi, I'm Nurse Duckworth. Would you mind if a student sits in on your appointment?'

'I doubt this could get more embarrassing so why not?'

'Checking your sexual health is not embarrassing. It is to be commended,' she said briskly.

We entered a small room, furnished with three seats, a small desk and an examination chair. In the corner sat a female student, pretty, attentive, no make-up, neat brown hair, eyes bright, not a flinch of cynicism flickering across her pleasant face. A few years of performing intimate inspections on the likes of me would soon knock that out of her.

I sat down facing Nurse Duckworth.

'OK, we're going to ask you a few questions about your recent sexual activity,' she said, picking up a clipboard from the desk.

'Is that necessary? Can't I just get the test and leave, please?'

'No, you'll be required to do this questionnaire first,' she said sternly.

'I'd rather not.'

'It provides vital information for tackling the problem of sexually transmitted infections in this country.'

'OK... OK,' I relented. 'I'll do it.'

'Are you in a long-term relationship?'

'I was but we broke up,' I directed my speech to the student. 'It wasn't my fault. She was... well, I know you shouldn't say crazy nowadays but...'

'Please just answer the questions, Mr Chichinadze. How many sexual partners have you had in the past year?'

'Two.'

'One was your ex-girlfriend.' Nurse Duckworth seemed to be writing more information than I was giving her. 'Who was the other?'

'A girl I met in a night club.' I turned back to the student. 'I don't usually do things like this.'

'Did you have full penetrative sex with this girl?'

'I think so. I was very drunk. She said we did.'

'Mr Chichinadze, you know it's not healthy to drink until you can't remember.'

'It depends what you are trying to forget.'

'Let's cut the questionnaire short.' Nurse Duckworth slapped her pen down, making it abundantly clear how tiresome patients like me were. 'Please get on the examination chair and lower your trousers.'

*

Afterwards, I sat on a bench in the square outside the hospital. Overhead, the September sun gave the final kiss of summer. In front of me, water trickled from a copper fountain into a green pool. Around it walked a man in a stripy jumper, arms longer than average, a wide grin on his face.

'Alright. It's pretty nice in there, isn't it?'

'Yes, Micky, it's the best hospital I've hung out in.'

'What was the test like?'

'Horrible.'

'Did you get the infamous questionnaire?'

I was unsure what type of person it was infamous with but answered anyway, 'Yes.'

'What's the damage then?'

'They don't think I've got anything. I've no symptoms and the swab was clear but I need to wait for the results to confirm.'

'Magic! I'm the same.' He held out a congratulatory hand that I refused to take. 'Look at us. We're just two players living the dream. Same time, same place, next Saturday?'

'I'm not doing that again.'

'How no?'

'It's not me. Plus when I told Liz she was very disappointed with me.'

'You mean when you telt Shell.'

'Why would I tell her? I couldn't care less what she thinks. I mean Liz.'

'Why's it any of Liz's business? You're single and had sex with someone who came after you. What's wrong with that?'

'She has a very high opinion of me and doesn't expect me to be going out doing things like this.'

'Does she no, aye? I tell you what, there is only one reason why she's raging.'

'What's that?'

'You must admit yous have a strange relationship. Matty's always bealing when he sees yous together.'

'I don't know why.'

'Me neither considering he doesnae know the hawf of it. There's no way she tells him about yous getting tickets for things, quaffing teas and all the other romantic stuff yous get up te.'

'I don't see what Matty's problem is.'

'I think his problem is it's obvious you're both in love with each other.'

Prickly needles dug into the left side of my chest. 'Who is that obvious to?'

'Everyone except you.'

'You've not mentioned this before, why are you saying it now?' I managed, feeling motion sick as my life hurtled past me.

'Why would I mention it to you? You're the one that should know it better than anyone.'

'Well, she now hates me.'

'And why do you think that is?'

'I told you. Because I slept with that girl...' I watched an army of ants disappear into the protection of their mound next to the leg of the bench. 'Well, I've done a lot more than that but –'

'The reason why she's annoyed at you is cos she's jealous.'

'As if someone like her would ever be interested in me.'

'She used to go out with Matty!'

'Yes but she explained that. You know that she's too nice for her own good. And he's got that whole tough guy thing going on....' I gripped the arm rest of the bench and swivelled to face Micky. 'Hang on. What do you mean that she *used* to go out with Matty?'

'They broke up. Surely she telt you that?'

'No.'

'Apparently, he's been knocking her around.'

'As in beating her up?'

The bruises on her wrists, her story about judo, the wrist bands at tennis, her voicemail, her limp in the house. She was trying to tell me all along. And I wouldn't listen. 'I've got to go.'

'No by yourself,' Micky said, his face stiffening. 'I've got a baseball bat and a snooker cue in the house.'

'What are you talking about?'

'I'm no letting you go after Matty yourself. He'll batter you senseless.'

'I'm not going to see him. I'm going to find Liz.'

He patted me on the back. 'Aye, go there first. You know what you've got to do.'

I did. But I had a few other things I also should have

done a long time ago to do first.

*

When I got to my desk Hugh was perching on the edge. 'Zezva, meet me on the fifth floor in five minutes.' His words were quiet but seemed loud. Loud in my head: loud in my heart.

Through the office to the Boardroom. Everything is fake. The ceiling is plasterboard and fake. The lights are halogen and fake; the windows are plastic and fake. Wires create fake networks of colleagues and clients. All fake but we won't notice because we are fake people with fake laughs and fake opinions.

On the fifth floor everything is real because that's where the clients go. The clients pay us real money. Some of us are paid a lot more real money than others. The boardroom table is made from real red oak. It was made by a real person called a carpenter. A carpenter made the chairs as well. Sitting in the boardroom makes you feel important or not important at all. If you're important you get your picture hung on the wall, until someone becomes more important than you and it gets taken it down. You aren't important the moment you don't hit your target or have lived for over sixty years.

Some people are never important.

Hugh sat at the red oak table, flanked by two men, their arms folded, faces stern, doing their best to create a tense atmosphere. The first man was sat upright, his suit jacket tugged up at the sleeves to reveal a gold watch and matching cufflinks. No artificial sparkle could take the attention from the ginger hair that sprouted from a cranium that was the shape of a cornflake box. He seemed very familiar - perhaps from a brochure or something. Next to him was sat an enormous man. He might have been leaning back, maybe he was sitting forward; it was impossible to tell. Moustache bristling, two fangs poking out his mouth, he breathed like a giant walrus.

Hugh introduced Cornflake Box Head as Mr Puntsent, the Senior Partner of the firm and the Walrus as Mr Kerr, the Head of HR.

'Zezva, please take a seat,' Hugh said.

Cornflakes and the Walrus sat unmoved, not even giving me the courtesy of the usual phoney greeting.

'I suspect that you know why you're here, Zezva. I must inform you that Mr Puntsent and Mr Kerr are attending this meeting as witnesses to this conversation.' Hugh intertwined his fingers and looked directly into my eyes. 'Let's get to the point. We're going to have to let you go I'm afraid,' he said, pretending to be regretful over a decision he'd been itching to make for months.

'On what grounds?'

'Gross misconduct. I have a quite extensive list.' Hugh dropped a bundle of papers onto the table with a thud. 'I won't read all the complaints out. I'll select a few. OK, pretending to be ill and then protesting against the firm's values upset a number of people around the office. Being involved in an attempted assault on myself was also inexcusable.' He licked his index finger and turned the page. 'Getting arrested and missing a morning of work costing us money in fees. Boasting of this indiscretion to clients in a later meeting. Taking this morning off without permission –'

'Hang on! This morning I legitimately went to the doctors.'

'You told Jayne you were going to the optician.'

'No I didn't. I told Jayne I was going to the dentists not the optician. She can't get anything right.'

I noticed Hugh was glancing at the other two pulling a *see what I mean* expression. 'But Zezva neither the dentist nor the optician is the doctors, which is where you're now claiming to have been.'

'Yes I know. But I was really at the doctors.'

'But you still lied,' he said slowly, like he was talking to someone very hard of thinking.

'Yes,' I said, matching his deliberate tone, 'but I told Jayne that to avoid embarrassment - not to get the morning off.'

'Embarrassment about what?'

'I went out on Saturday night and met this girl. I thought she'd given me a disease so I went to the GUM clinic. I'm not exactly going to be shouting that around the office, am I?'

No, I thought, not when I can save the story for special occasions like this: in a meeting with the head of my department, firm and HR.

'The GUM clinic?' said Hugh, probably more convinced than ever that I was clinically insane. 'Do you think this is helping your cause? You're admitting having a drink problem; you're admitting to being promiscuous; you're admitting to catching diseases and, worst of all, lying again.'

'Hey slow down there with the allegations. I don't have a drink problem. Where did you get that from? And I don't have a disease,' I turned to the Walrus, who was scribbling away. 'Get that down: medical proof of no diseases.'

'I notice you didn't deny being promiscuous?' said Hugh, unable to control his lawyerish urge to find a flaw in my argument.

'Even if I was promiscuous, which I don't concede, I'm sure there isn't a clause prohibiting that in my employment contract,' I said, in a half-hearted attempt to lawyer him back.

'Look, I know you are a peculiar person. I knew that when I took you on but you were bright and I thought I'd take a risk. But in a year and a half here you haven't changed a bit. It's pathetic the lack of loyalty you have to this firm and our goals. It's one of the many strange things about you.'

I sat forward and rested my forearms on the table. 'What other strange things, Hugh?'

Hugh flicked his hand in dismissal. 'Not enough time. Anyway you'll receive a neutral reference and we'll recommend a good counsellor. I hope you understand that we are being more than fair.'

'I understand more than you think.'

'Good. OK, start to clear your desk. You can leave right away.'

'You think that I'm crazy but I'm not. It's you. All of you.'

'Yes, Zezva, the world is crazy and you're the only normal one,' said the Cornflake Box headed Senior Partner, his voice plumy and conceited.

'Well Mr Kelloggs I imagine you're quite pleased with the way the world is. But I'm not,' I said looking deep into his eyes. 'You know, in five hundred years they will look back on this age and say, human beings went mad. When everything was ruined by us chasing the things we didn't need. The time when we ate steak from Argentina when there were cows ten miles away. You know, when we ruin this planet and the apocalypse comes and mankind is living in caves, we'll fight a war not for greed but for want. Why? Because there will be nothing left. And the kids will say, "But they knew what was happening, why did they do it?" And the answer is people like me towing the line and accepting what people like you tell me to do. Well I'm never doing it again.'

'What are you talking about?' Hugh said.

'You're the greediest people in the age of greed. It's destroying us. You work all day and night and at weekends and for what? For money you don't need. There is no point in you. If you died tomorrow all your clients would just employ someone else. People would come to your funeral to network and they wouldn't come at all if it was raining. You think you're rich but you're the poorest people around.'

As I walked out I heard Hugh ask the others, 'Why was he talking about funerals and Argentinean cows?'

'It's really sad - he's obviously lost it,' Cornflakes replied.

*

I stood outside and took in a deep breath and felt like I exhaled months of tension when I breathed it out. I know sometimes I partake in a bit of self loathing but if I didn't fit in, in a place like that then maybe I wasn't that bad after all.

I searched the street for a taxi so I could go to Liz's house. I couldn't see any passing. I took out my phone from the inner pocket of my suit jacket to call one and saw that I had a voicemail. I dialled and put the handset to my ear.

'Hi, it's Shell. Look Zezva I can't believe what happened the other night. I'm so, so sorry. I...' Her voice cracked and she broke off. 'I never thought it would end like this.'

I actually took the phone away from my ear and stared at it like it was a foreign object. Was I actually hearing Shell apologising? I re-started the message and listened again. She was. And she also went on to say, 'You know I thought you were so amazing when I first met you. You still are. I wanted you to, I don't know, channel all that intelligence and bitterness and energy into something positive. I thought you were wasted in that job. But I know... I know now what it must have been like me going on at you but I've been so frustrated and suffocated and hurt this year and I couldn't take it anymore. I know when you attacked Sparky it wasn't you and maybe I drove you to it. But what happened on Saturday night with the knife you drove me to as well. But I regret it so much. I wanted to really hurt you. I admit it. And that scared me because... well... even though we're wrong and this whole thing has been wrong, I care for you so much. I don't want us to hate each other. I told my dad everything that happened. Things are better between us. He told me how kind you were about me that day in the restaurant. Thanks for that. OK. Right. Bye.'

I stood there and thought about her and smiled. Although my earlier speech to Hugh and his cronies could have been a bit more profound, I knew Shell would have been proud of me. A taxi passed with its light on. I hailed it, got inside and asked for where I knew she'd be. I wiped away the moisture that had formed on my upper lip and stared ahead.

After twenty minutes, we pulled up outside Ricky's. I got out and noticed Sparky's red sports car parked outside as I went in. Head lowered, I wove through those wooden tables and chairs.

I stopped where I knew they'd be. My chin rose and levelled. Oblivious to me as ever, they perched on a single bean bag. Shell and Sparky. Not hugging. Not kissing. But eating each others' faces off.

I stamped my foot on the stone floor, the thud of my heel jerking them out of their embrace. They both looked up. Horror. Pure horror on their faces.

'Zezva, what are you doing here?' Shell was on her feet tugging her clothes back into position 'This isn't how it looks.'

I let out a low, deep laugh. 'Of course it's how it looks!'

'Zezva,' she wailed, following me through the bar and out the door.

I saw the taxi hadn't left yet and re-flagged it.

The 'Zezvas' and 'stops' and 'pleases' ceased and three words remained, a pleaded, 'Please say something.'

I reached the taxi and turned to face her. 'Like what?'

'Please know nothing happened with Sparks until you and I were over.'

'Shell, it doesn't matter.'

'You don't mean that.'

'I do. I'm pleased for you.'

'You don't mean that either.'

'I really do. Message me when you're coming round to the house to get the rest of your things and I'll go out so you don't need to see me. If there's anything that you are unsure of who owns it, you keep it. But make sure you leave the Dog. I want him to stay.'

She nodded, disturbing the tears that had formed in her eyes.

I gripped the handle of the taxi door and lowered it.

Her green nailed hand clasped my forearm. 'Where are you going?'

'To see Liz.'

'Are you with her?'

'Not yet.'

The tears now drowned her beautiful dark eyes and she smiled with genuine joy. She was free.

I got in the taxi and watched her as it pulled away. I knew I'd never see her again.

*

I knew where I needed to go and what I had to do but first I needed to do something I should have done a long time before.

I went home and into my bedroom and pulled a shoebox out from under the bed. I rummaged inside until I found a letter addressed to Zviad Chichinadze, my grandfather. The same letter I wrote when my mother died. I was going to mail that letter and tell that miserable old man who had deserted us what a disgrace he was.

Then I stopped and realised that, of course, my grandfather cared that my mother had died and that his disinterest was fake. Deep inside he cried like I cried but he couldn't show it because of his pride. The same pride that had led him to force my mother to leave her home and country. Pride that would poison him to the end of his days. My anger dissipated and I pitied that irritable, red faced wine-drinker of my earliest memories.

I ripped up the letter and sat on my bed and I thought back to the night in Ricky's where this whole thing had started and thought how scared I'd been. I was scared of losing my job and my girlfriend and alienating the few allies I had. And in a few short days I'd managed that and more. I'd been beaten up, thrown through a window, arrested and imprisoned. I'd slept with a stranger, been tested for diseases, had a knife thrown at me and my possessions destroyed. I'd offended everyone from my boss to policemen, nurses to football coaches.

But despite it all I felt unbelievably, unreservedly happy. I'd made myself miserable striving for all the things I didn't want in the first place. Now I had nothing but the one thing I didn't have before: hope.

*

Across the panorama of life, the changing vista of reality, to a meeting, perhaps a realisation. Gazing up at the tapestry of the heavens Two billows fuse; a cloud like Georgia. The clouds had been peach the night we spent in the park. Maybe they would be again.

The eye levels. People flit by, ethereal figures, phantoms in my midst, phantoms in my mind. The wind picks up and chills. It is now September. The birds would be leaving soon. We all would.

The journey is soon over. And here I am. Up the stairwell, each step juddering through my body. Somehow I reach the top. Real nerves: not painful or sweat inducing but a feeling nestling somewhere within. A soft tap on the door. The sound of keys. My breath sharpens. It opens. A woman. A faint light kissing her delicate features, unmarked but for the speckle of her beauty. Eyes locking, feeling that something again; so hard to find; impossible to explain. She dissolves into my arms.

She releases me and takes my hand and we go into the living room. We clasp each other and I speak.

'Liz, I heard what Matty did. You tried to tell me...' A gust of regret takes my breath away. 'Are you OK?'

She nods and clasps my hand tighter.

'I know you think I don't care. But I do...' I can't stop swallowing but I've started so I must finish. 'I've lost the most important person in my life once before. I can't let it happen again.'

A ringing in the distance.

I ignore it and keep talking perhaps scared of what she'll say. 'I don't know why I haven't told you before. I was too scared to admit it. Even to myself. But I don't expect anything. We can keep on being friends and that's fine. But I love you. I always have.'

She shakes in my arms. 'You're the most pessimistic person I've ever met.'

I exhale deeply and know where this is going.

'You're so perceptive when it comes to bad things. You notice every ulterior motive, devious act, bit of hypocrisy.'

The ringing goes on like the sound of a bell.

'But you don't notice anything positive. You think everyone else is blind but you're the one that can't see any good.'

'I'll leave,' I mumble. I release her and turn towards the door. She grabs my hand and draws me back towards her.

'You're really stupid aren't you?'

'Anything else?'

'Yes. You're weird and anxious and self-involved and

angry. But I've loved you from the moment I met you. I never wanted to be with Matty. I wanted to be with you,' she says, her words rising above the now persistent ringing.

I want to ask her how she could be so forgiving and to tell her that I didn't deserve it. Then I smile because I've done exactly what she'd said: gone straight for the negative.

She hazes in front of me and I forget everything else and instead take in her words and they seem too perfect to be true.

We hold each other and release all that pent up passion with a rich, urgent kiss. A thumping in the distance grows stronger drowned out by the throbbing beat of my heart.

A crunching sound followed by a tremendous thwack. Thunderous footsteps.

The final brush of her silken flesh. Fleeting. Tender. Over.

A spark in my eye; a crunching blow to my temple. A semi-conscious plunge, unable to cushion my fall, my head hits against floorboards.

The scream of, 'Matty, Matty, stop it.'

I open one eye and see Liz holding him back.

I clamber to my feet. He pushes Liz aside and faces me, his eyes fierce and determined. A moment of calm follows. Blood pours from my temple as I steady myself and gather all my fading strength. He charges.

Controlled by that something else, I move out the way, trailing my leg, tripping him and sending him crashing to the floor. He falls awkwardly and looks hurt. He crawls into the hall to regroup but I follow and dive onto his torso and smother him down before he can get up.

But he's so much stronger than me and pushes me off.. We scramble to our feet. Remembering the murder in his eyes, I gather the remains of my dignity, my pride and my strength and charge at him. I drive him out the front door towards the banister of the stairwell. We deflect off it and he uses his weight to force me back. Pinned against the wall, a boulder-like head crushes into my face, chiselling me into submission.

I can hear Liz screaming at him to leave me alone but he's not listening. Dense fists quarry into my abdomen. An upper cut crunches into the bones in my nose, the pain sharp and instant. He draws back, lines up my already crushed face with his slab-like fist.

'MATTY NO!' Liz grabs at his arm.

He roars and swats her away with a flailing arm. She staggers back and teeters on the edge of the stairs. A timeless impasse, a prayer unanswered, she falls, her head jolting as she rebounds off each step. And there she lies, resting at the bottom of the stairs, blood forming around her head, her turquoise eyes rolling up towards eternity.

People celebrate and depress themselves over landmarks, but you don't remember things like the change between 20s and 30s. It is events that separate your life. I remember my life before and after that moment. When I had Liz and when I didn't. When we shared our love for a fleeting moment. When not a breath later, she was gone.

EPILOGUE

In the days that followed I was overcome by a sadness that wouldn't go away. I could still see the blue flashing lights, the men in green overalls leaning over her, their ears pressed against her chest.

I went to the police station. Cells, interviews, questions. Finally I was allowed to leave. The words, 'You are released pending the victim regaining consciousness,' inscribed into my memory forever.

I got home and collapsed onto the couch and gave in. That's when I sent a message to everyone saying I'd left to live in Georgia and wouldn't be in contact again. With that, I barricaded myself inside the house. Occasionally the door bell would buzz; a few times someone knocked at the door. I'd get scared and my body would tremble and I'd calm only when they went away.

Soon the calls stopped. I turned off my modem and

phone. I'd given up on the world. It seemed like it had given up on me.

At first I sat in the living room, amongst the furniture left by a dead mum and aunt, ripped and shredded by the girl who had never cared for me like they did.

All those hours, the Dog stayed close, his body slumped next to me. I opened the door so he could taste the freedom I couldn't face myself but he didn't leave.

A week later he did escape from me and everything else. I got up to see him lying still in his basket, his water and food left untouched. I had no explanation why other than he was gone, like everyone else in my life.

I took him down to the garden at the back of my flat and dug a hole behind the pear tree. I lowered his carcass into the hole and dropped the soil over the blanket that was wrapped around his body. I thought of my mother's funeral and the wind and the pall bearers. I thought of that day and this and I told myself it was a dog and it couldn't compare to my mother's death and, of course, the Dog wasn't my only friend.

My sleep problems worsened during that time. I lay awake for what seemed like hours, watching the shadows creeping across the ceiling. Time drifted before my eyes, across the lost days and long nights. Soon the copper glow of autumn dropped into the blackness of winter.

One morning I felt stabbing pains in my stomach and couldn't breathe. I thought I was going to die and stumbled to the landline phone but it had been disconnected. I dragged myself out the flat and into the hallway.

When I regained consciousness I was in hospital. I'd been found by a neighbour. I was put on a drip and ordered to rest. When the doctors found out that I'd been hiding in my house for two months they advised me to visit Dr O'Brien upon my discharge. If I refused, the doctor said, 'they may need to take appropriate action.'

I didn't know what this action was but I didn't like the sound of it. So I went to see Dr O'Brien twice a week. I found his questions tiresome. He insisted on talking about my childhood and my mother and didn't seem interested in what had happened last summer. When I brought it up he kept saying we would get to it.

When we did *get to it*, I couldn't speak about those days without getting upset. So instead Dr O'Brien asked me to go away and write about it. This gave me a new purpose and I felt better. I lay in bed and wrote for hours at a time, sometimes staying up all night and writing into the early morning.

When O'Brien read it he asked me how Liz was – there was a deep concern in his voice.

I said that I didn't know. I was too scared to find out.

I think that when he put his hand on my shoulder and stared into my eyes that he forgot he was a Doctor or eminent or esteemed. He told me to face my problems when they arose and not to hide from them. And most importantly he told me to go away and find out what had happened to Liz.

I said I couldn't take the risk. What if she was dead? Or paralysed?

He said that she wouldn't be.

I said, that was a guess. A kind guess. But a guess. My only hope was that she was OK. If I found out that she wasn't, I'd have nothing.

'Has she not contacted you?' O'Brien said.

'I don't know. My phone and internet is cut off. I don't answer the door.'

He wrote very quickly after I told him that, which scared me.

I made some excuse and said I had to go.

O'Brien stood up and shook my hand before I left. He hadn't done that before.

I think he knew that I wasn't going to go back.

From then on I stopped trying to sleep. In the light and in the dark, I waited on the sofa. I don't know what I was waiting for but I knew it would come. Finally, I heard the door being broken down. A figure burst into the room. It strode across the floor and pushed open the curtains. A young, heroic man stood in the dim room. It was you, Micky. It was you.

You sat there and read my words, stopping occasionally to make us drinks or go out and get some food. As you read you laughed sometimes. You shook your head others. Sometimes your face became stern and your breathing more pronounced. You didn't stop or ask me any questions or dispute what I'd written. I appreciated that. You only spoke once to slag off my depiction of your accent. You were smiling when you said it. I know I wrote some things about you that were a bit negative and was worried about that when you were reading it. When you made a joke about the accent thing that made me feel so much better.

When you finished reading, you released a deep sigh and rested the folder against the window sill.

*

Micky comes across the room and sits down next to me on the couch, despair dulling his usually lively green eyes. 'Right first of all let me tell you about Liz...'

'No,' I snap. 'Not yet.'

'How no?'

'I'm not ready. That's why. So don't even –'

'Alright, alright, cool your beans. We'll leave it. For now...' Micky says softly. 'Let's talk about something else then... like what a midden this place is.'

Micky walks to the ledge and yanks the window open, the fresh snap of the winter air battling the stagnation of the room. A draft runs through the house, kicking the broken front door back and forth, its busted hinges creaking.

'So you lied when you said you were goin to Georgia?' a harsh texture to his words. 'Do you know how many times I've been round here and called ye? Then I seen your neighbour the now and he says they took you away to hospital no that long ago and he's no seen ye since. Thank God I knocked that door down.'

'Sorry.'

'Never mind your sorrys.' He picks up the folder from the window sill, strides across the room and sits back down next to me on the couch. 'Are you alright? You're so thin.'

I shrug.

'Come on talk to us. What have you been doing for the past three months?'

'Sitting in here. Writing that.'

'But why?'

'I couldn't face it any longer. It's quieter in here. Dark. No people. Less worries.'

'Zezva, there isnae a worry in the world that's more worrying than ending up like this.'

'Maybe.' I take the pages I've written from Micky and put them back in their folder. They look out of order, which irritates me but I don't say anything. I can rearrange them when I get him to leave. 'Look, it's nice of you to come round but I'm fine...'

'No, you're no! You're the least fine person I've seen. Look at the state of you.'

'I'll come out again in a couple of weeks.'

'Did you say that to yourself a couple of weeks back?'

'Maybe.'

'Well, there is no way any pal of mine is gonee live like this. Nae chance. I take this as a personal offence. I'm coming to live here for a while cos you cannae be trusted by yourself. No argument.'

I look at his face and it's tense and contains none of its usual exuberance. 'OK,' I relent. 'But on one condition. You don't make me talk about what happened to Liz. If you do I'll ask you to leave.'

'Fine, but I'm no leaving till you sort yourself out and you're happy again.'

'Micky, you can't make someone else happy. They can only do it themselves.'

'What do you mean I cannae? Of course I can.'

He storms out the door that he'd broken down to get in. I hear his van screeching outside. He is soon back, with an enormous black bag slung over his shoulder. He chucks the bag on the floor, takes out his phone, cancels all his jobs and embraces his new profession: amateur psychologist. He goes about cheering me up in the only way he knows how. He buys takeaway, makes coffees, keeps the windows wide open, insisting he likes the fresh air, his teeth chattering as he shivers through his protestations. As I watch his big-hearted, kind stupidity I almost find it to be cure in itself.

When I want to go to bed, he stops me. 'You're no going to bed yet. The American Football is on.'

Into the cold night Micky's constant, furious pursuit of life never dims. Not when the curtains flap in the icy breeze or when his team starts to lose.

Then finally he falls asleep, exhausted by his efforts, his mouth upturned, his body fidgeting with the excitement of being a few hours away from waking up and starting life all over again. Perhaps his spirit reassures me or maybe it's just his presence, but either way I find sleep, deep and quiet, awaking in the late morning the next day to the smell of burnt bacon, drilled wood and paint. Micky is in the hall whistling tunelessly.

'What are you doing?'

'Fixing the door,' he shouts. 'Food in the kitchen.'

During the cold afternoons we watch DVDs; long, daft, uneventful comedies, that Micky had obviously brought to make me laugh. And when three movies in, I start to smile, a glint of happiness forms, which spreads to Micky's angelic face.

'I knew this would work,' he says, jiggling in the chair.

But it didn't work. He did. I've no idea what the movies were about because Micky talked the entire way through every one. And that's what made me smile more than anything.

The more films we watch, the more excited he gets; the more caffeine he drinks, the more he talks. He rises every two minutes, going to the fridge, opening cupboards, closing doors, popping in, going out. He howls with laughter at the jokes, does impressions of the characters, misunderstands the non-existent plots. And all his theories and stories and opinions come out in a constant stream of consciousness. He doesn't wear a watch because only losers are on time. He saw a woman spitting the other day and knew she would be good in bed; women that have no manners always are. He read a story about a man who had a tree growing out of his arm. He expects to go to heaven because though he's let down a lot of girls he's never lied to or disrespected any of them.

I hope his twisted utilitarian God will forgive me as well.

I know when I open my eyes that today Micky has to go back to work. I sit watching him pack his things into his bag and want to ask him to stay but I can't; I've already embarrassed myself enough. Perhaps sensing my thoughts Micky is thoughtful, 'Why don't you come oot with me today? That way you're no in the hoose all alone. Plus I'd like it if you came along,' he says, blushing a little.

'I don't know if I'm ready to see anyone yet.'

'You won't have to. I only have a couple of jobs, they're way out West. You can stay in the van or wait in a café.'

'Well OK then. If you don't mind?'

'One condition.'

'What?'

'Go have a shower, change your clothes and shave. You look like a jake.'

I enter the bathroom and stare into the mirror. A weak, thin man faces me; skin hanging from his bones, the last remnants of youth disappearing from his yellowing face. I pull my top off and gasp at the semi-circles of bone that protrude from my chest. I lather my face and an old blunt razor out the cabinet. With it I shear through my beard with slow, painful strokes.

I shower and put on the only clean clothes in my drawer. I go to the front door and open it, I force my way through the breach, closing it before I can change my mind. My hand trembles as I fit the new key into the lock. I step down the stairs, my legs readjusting to the unusual feeling of motion and the twinkling awakening of my muscles.

Outside, Micky is spraying and scraping the ice off the windscreen of his rusty white van. I clamber into the passenger seat, kicking all the bottles and crisp packets aside.

Forty minutes later we arrive at the job. Micky addresses me parentally, 'Right go and wait in that café over there. They do a cracking breakfast.'

Inside the café, I order a tea and some toast. The other customers seem different to how I remember people: bigger, louder, more confident. Seeing the whites of their eyes and their meaty hands and thick hair and sturdy arms I think that I must be ill from staying in the house too long and that my lack of vitamin D might mean I'm going blind or something like that. I run my tongue around my cracked lips and feel thin and unhealthy.

At one o'clock Micky comes to collect me, apologising for taking so long. We order a late lunch which we eat in the van - two crusty white rolls dipped into steaming tomato soup.

'When are you coming back to play football?' Micky

says..

'You know I can't.'

'Everyone keeps on asking about ye. Even Ethel misses you. She was saying you were her favourite player. I think her memory is getting dodgy in her old age, mind.'

'You know I can't come back.'

'Matty doesnae play anymere. None of us wanted him back,' he said, lowered his voice. 'Not after what happened.'

'Which was my fault,' I say.

'It was all his fault. It came out he'd been beating her up for ages.'

'Yes and Liz tried to tell me and I ignored her.'

'No, she didnae. She hinted and you didnae pick up on it. You didnae do that on purpose. The reason he was so raging that time he came round and yous got into that fight was cos she'd telt him she liked you and didn't want to be with him anymere.'

I try not to smile. I don't know why the comment about her liking me still felt so good, even after all that had happened.

'Micky, how can I face those people when they know what I did?' I say, trying to avoid facing the truth a moment longer.

'Why would you be bothered about facing them?! Are you scared of being congratulated? He attacked you and you held your own, defending yourself and Liz.'

'I can't face hearing what happened to her. She was the only person in all that mess that did nothing wrong.' He opens his mouth but I silence him by holding up my hand. 'Please, don't talk about her.'

'Do you no care what happened to her after the fall?'

'Micky, of course I care what happened!' I pause and try to control myself but can't remember the last time a question has annoyed me so much.

'Well, you arenae exactly –'

'Listen, she was lying in a pool of blood; they carried her away unconscious on a stretcher; they needed four paramedics to lift her. I didn't know if she'd recover. When I sorted all that police stuff out, I hid from the truth. That's the only way I can cope with things. I thought she might be dead. I couldn't face hearing those words. Not after my mum. Not again. I would rather never leave the house again.'

'Deid?! You've been sitting in that hoose thinking she could be deid and she's fine.'

'What do you mean she's fine?' I say, grabbing the sleeve of Micky's blue overall.

'Get off me.' He shakes his arm free. 'She's a hunded per cent fine. She was unconscious for a while and had a bad concussion but when she got over that in the end all she did was break her wrist and get some stitches in the back of her heid.'

'Really?'

'Aye. So that's why you've been lying to everyone and hiding in your hoose cos you thought she was either deid or paralysed?'

'Yes.'

'You're a fucking idiot.' Micky starts thumping his fist off the steering wheel and growls in pure frustration.

I join in and slam the heel of my hand off the dashboard.

The van shakes and we must look like we've escaped from the zoo.

Our eyes meet. 'I should just punch you,' Micky says.

'Go for it.'

'Nah, that's what you want. You're no the victim here so I'm no gonee make you one.'

The fact he knows me so well makes me want to smile and although I try to hide it, I must give it away a bit because the tension drops and we both sit back in our seats.

'Jesus Christ, Zezva. Can you fuck this up anymere? Liz telt me she's been sending you an email every week and you havenae replied.'

'No, they cut my phone and internet off.'

'I seen her last week. She believed that bullshit about you moving back to Georgia. She thinks you've moved away cos you blame her for what happened with Matty and cos you don't want to speak to her again.'

'Why would she think that?'

'I have no idea. What she should think is that you're a selfish wee prick and no better than Matty.'

I wound down the window and took a breath of the crisp winter air. 'You're right...'

'Aye, I am.' He lifts his hand to hit the steering wheel again but pauses mid strike and slowly lowers it like he doesn't have the energy. 'Take my phone and ring her right now and beg her to forgive you or come up with a good lie because if you lose her...'

'I'll drink my soup first,' I said, reaching for the cup holder.

He slaps away my hand. 'No, you won't.'

'How do you know she still wants to hear from me?'

'I don't! Ring her and find out.'

'I'll do it outside.'

'How?'

'I don't want you to hear.'

I take the phone, open the door, get out and walk around the front of the van. I check both ways. However hard I look I can't see any traffic. I cross the road and shelter in a doorway.

Five minutes later I return to the van.

'Well?' Micky asks.

'It went well.'

'Did it?' he scrolls through his phone. 'Sure it did. The last call isn't her number.'

I pick up my now cold soup and take a drink. 'She doesn't answer her mobile in the day so I called her work.'

He frowns and looks dubious but says, 'What did you say?'

'I explained everything.'

'And are you going to meet her?'

'Yes.'

'Whereaboots?'

'Somewhere in the park. She said she'd find me.'

Micky screwed up his features. 'She'll find you in a park?'

'Yes.'

'What park?'

'Regents Park.'

'When?'

'Now.'

'Alright. I'll drive you there then.'

We pull up outside the park and he dulls the engine. We sit in silence, both facing forwards, the moisture from our breath steaming up the windscreen. Micky breaks the impasse, his voice deeper and slightly croaky, 'OK,' he says and swallows. 'You'd best go.'

I get out and walk around the van to the pavement. Micky winds down the window and sticks his head out. 'Zezva, don't do anything stupid.'

I nod and walk away, turning to catch a last glance of Micky sitting alone in his van. He looks tired perhaps even defeated.

I pass through the black gate of the park and follow the trail. The tarmac path is hard under my feet, the frost twinkling in the fading light. As the road dips deep into the vale, a surge of cold shivers across the silver blades of the grass.

I reach the basin where the common meets the lake and follow the curve of the shoreline. A wind blows through the leafless trees, biting into my face. The birds have all departed now; the wooden rowing boats taken away too. To think that beyond the many horizons the sun shimmers; just like it had six months before on this very same path.

I arrive at the jetty and continue towards the water, the boards guiding me to the edge. The jetty dips into the water. Drifts of ice cut across the lake, tickled by the drooping willow branches that brush the grey surface.

I gaze up to face the final glow of the afternoon extinguished by the winter night. A moment passes before a flicker of redemption comes from the light of the moon, an ivory flame penetrating the thick clouds. And with it the heavens come to life, wild shadows in the dark sky, crafting together, cutting apart, plotting yet distrusting.

The stillness breaks and it starts to snow, faintly at first, but growing heavier. A thousand thick, white flakes, drifting down and nestling on the ground. Then the tears come. Soft tears for the lost days that won't return; for every friend I've lost and never had; for the Georgian woman with no home; for the most wanted unwanted dog and for the girl lying at the bottom of the stairs.

The snow continues to fall, on my face and on the land, on the trees and on the grey waters that lap against the bank. A line of mooring posts drop into the distance. An old rope is tied round the nearest post, noosing its rotting neck. Next to it lays a fallen tree, dying in the lake, its roots still clinging to the verge. I stand at the edge and look at the water below. Tightening the scarf around my neck, I pull the gloves above my wrists.

All the timelessness of the past months lifts and I feel each second pass. Then I sense a movement, a sense of being. I turn. A person, silhouetted and still. Twenty feet away. Then she drops her hood, only the glint of her eyes and strands of her golden hair visible in the moonlight.

We begin to walk towards each other but stop before we are close enough to touch. The contours of her face change and her cheeks rise: that smile; that other-worldly smile touching me with its bliss, yet again. I go to her and we hold each other. I believe what she told me on the phone that she forgave me. I know my apologies can't change what I've done but now as I grip her arms and look into her eyes, the truth stares back and with it flows the love we feel that won't go away.

As the moon drops behind a cloud, a glossy blackness envelops us and the rest of the world is gone.

THE END

www.ingramcontent.com/pod-product-compliance
Lightning Source LLC
Chambersburg PA
CBHW021031130626
46552CB00005B/1790